I0574982

OWEN HOLT

Normalheroes

Heroism Redefined

This novel is entirely a work of fiction. The names, characters and incidents portrayed in it are the work of the author's imagination. Any resemblance to actual persons, living or dead, events or localities is entirely coincidental.

Owen Holt asserts the moral right to be identified as the author of this work.

First edition

ISBN: 979-8-9995425-0-2

Cover art by nerdy.ness

This book was professionally typeset on Reedsy.
Find out more at reedsy.com

Dedicated to my parents and my church, who showed me what heroism looks like in the hardest time.

Contents

Foreword		iii
1	Prologue: Normalheroes	1
2	Soar	5
3	Normalvillains	8
4	Cursed	11
5	Nighthawk	13
6	This Time	16
7	Quiet	18
8	Songheroes	20
9	Mistakes	25
10	King	27
11	Mortal	30
12	Heroes 1.0	33
13	Aliveheroes	43
14	Rise	47
15	Raven	51
16	Stillhawk	53
17	Memories	57
18	Burnt	59
19	Fractures	61
20	Fall	64
21	Skyscraper	67
22	Heroes 2.0	69
23	Fate	89

24 Architect   97
25 Ashes   101
The Hideout   111

Foreword

My philosophy for living life is to always try to be a hero. Heroes mess up and make mistakes, but heroes get back on track and try to fix things. Heroes step in to help other people. Heroes shoulder burdens.

The heroes contained in this story aren't your typical Hollywood style. They're normal people in masks, who deal with deeply human emotions and pain in extraordinary settings.

I did this to try to define something really important to me. What is a hero, exactly? How do I define heroism?

I think you'll find each of these stories either suggests a new definition of heroism, or challenges an old one. Each story is crafted in a way to show what heroes are really like, as real people just trying their hardest to be the hero of their story.

I strive to always be the hero. I hope you will too.

Before you start, though, I just have one question.

How do you define heroism?

1

Prologue: Normalheroes

How can you go from restrained to limitless in the blink of an eye?

I'd spent my life studying the heroes of the world around me—from those gifted with incredible gifts to those making the most of what they had. The rope that strung them together had evaded me for quite some time.

Finally. It was within my grasp.

For a time, I had believed it was some ancient prophecy. Whispers of the Chosen Ones had excited me, caused me to go deep into the underground of cities in order to find out more.

But what I had found didn't line up. They were just lies.

The Chosen Ones were gifted with power. But what of the powerless?

There were many, weak and powerless, who had changed so many lives. One had changed my own, so many years ago. He'd started this quest for answers. These people had taken the world that was dealt them. The same horrible hand we'd all been given. And they'd played it not for their benefit, but for others.

How could they not be chosen? How could they not be just as

powerful as those superhumans?

For a time, I'd believed it was courage. This was closer to the true answer, but not quite there. I'd realized the fear they went through. I'd realized the strength it took to get through it all. And that was an important facet, for sure.

But I'd met those who told me there wasn't something in them that caused them to continue. Mere mortals in a world of superhumans—who were they to think they could do it alone? Who were they to think they were the catalyst?

Again and again, these mere mortals were the shifting factor in my theories. I refused to accept they weren't heroes—I'd seen them do more heroic deeds than those blessed with powers. I'd seen a millionaire giving back to the poor. I'd seen a firefighter stepping in to save the lives of children, only ancient gear serving to protect him. I'd seen police give their lives to protect the ideals of justice and peace that we all hunted.

And I'd seen those "Chosen Ones" betray the world. I'd seen them sink ships and destroy cities. I'd seen them battle it out with no care for the human life.

I'd begun to suspect these mortals held a different kind of power.

The superhumans? They could trust themselves to finish the job. They were strong enough.

But sometimes they couldn't trust in their power. They couldn't trust they had the *mental* strength to resist the corruption of power and might.

They were forced to make horrible decisions because of the burden placed on them. They were responsible for the lives of billions.

And several had succumbed to the pressure. Understandably— they weren't horrible people, but they were lashing out at this world that expected so much of them because of how they were born.

Those who had remained were hollow. Wounded beyond belief. So hurt that sometimes they struggled to see the good in anyone, let alone themselves.

But I'd seen the mortals with the will of gods. I'd seen them step up beside their heroes, encouraging them, showing them the good, and fighting beside them. They weren't partial; they would defend their fellow man whether he had powers or not for as long as they could.

These were the ones that saved the world.

Even if they didn't have flashy powers or if they didn't fight off alien intruders (although some did), these were the ones that kept everyone going. They saved lives. They kept the more powerful of us alive and willing to protect.

After years of searching, I ended in a battlefield. It was empty now, but it had been torn apart by the throes of war only a short time before.

I met a soldier there, one who had fought with the superheroes. A hero in his own right. A warrior in this endless struggle for good.

And that was the secret.

He stood up, dusted off his uniform, and blinked away a few last tears for his comrades. "We won," he whispered softly. "*We won.*"

"But how?" The battlefield, although solemn, struck me with a sense of awe. These odds had seemed insurmountable. An army of the strongest of those fallen heroes, "supervillains", as some called them, had risen against the people and the good.

But even as our heroes died, new ones arose. The kind that would be unexpected to someone unlike me—someone who hadn't studied this as I had. I knew that these heroes were sometimes the most powerful.

And after the last superhero fell, normalheroes took her place. These men had stood for what was good. They had stood for justice. They had stood for peace.

"We stood for hope." He glanced at the setting sun. "That's what brings us through. The fact that even if we die, things will be better." A deep sigh. "Many of us died, but it's better for them now. And it's better for me." He dropped his gun in the dirt, turned, and walked off.

Hope. That *fit*, I realized. Hope could inspire courage. Hope could gift that strength to overcome the struggles. And hope was what had been ripped away from the supervillains and heroes alike. The heroes clung to its remains, a buoy in the storm.

But the villains had forsaken it. They'd been faced with the pressure, and they'd fought for good once upon a time, but when the world had continued to pound down on them, they'd lost it. Lost that vision of the future.

That was what separated the heroes and the villains.

2

Soar

When I first donned the cloak, it felt odd.

Until I felt the wind racing through my hair as I swung through the streets. Then it felt normal.

That first night was one of new promises, new realities, and new dreams. A night of optimism and hope. A night of power for the powerless.

My abilities? Zero. My talent? None.

All I had was a deeper sense of purpose.

For months I'd trained myself, practicing routines day and night. Practice, then breakfast; ten minutes of practice, then work; two hours of practice, a quick dinner, then sleep. Every day, for six months, I practiced.

After all, practice would make perfect.

Practice would make me.

Within three months, I could fly. The blades I'd affixed to chains became a language for me, a silent poem as I calculated the movements that would carry me through the city like a bird. Anchoring points became privy to a second sense. I soared like an eagle.

I was becoming a hero.

I had to. Because I was stronger.

Not physically. Where everyone else had superhuman abilities, I had only human ones. Where everyone else could take a shot and be back the next day, I had to suffer.

But the suffering made me stronger. I could get back up. And I did. The suffering made me something different from them.

Suffering didn't make me a superhero. It made me a human hero.

And the city needed one.

Without humanity, superheroes risked everything in each moral decision. Every choice they made affected thousands. Every off day killed people. Every loss they took upon themselves. It was understandable that they'd lose their humanity.

I prayed I never would. I'd be the hero. The human hero.

I watched the city burn from my windows after the second attack from the self-proclaimed Emperor Arsonist. Smoke filled the sky and hid the sun. The screams of innocents filled the air. Pain hovered like a bitter taste on my tongue.

The city needed heroes. So I started training.

We had heroes. But they were preoccupied. Bigger threats, bigger monsters. When the fate of the country was at sake, why would you prioritize Salde City?

I prioritized it because for me, it was home.

And you fought for home. Every time.

So I would be the hero.

I fought for my community, because I suffered with them. Detachment was impossible when every loss you let happen echoed through the town. When every failure etched in stone a reminder. When everyone you helped stood on the streets beside you.

6

So I fought to be the human hero they needed.

Each twirl of the blade, each miss, each hit, it shaped me. It formed the figure I wanted to be.

The first time I stepped out into the night, blue cloak donned, hood up, I felt the shattered heartbeat of a city in the air. Within minutes of soaring through city streets, I felt my own break at the scream of a young woman. It pierced the night like a siren, breaking the peace. When I arrived, my weapons seemed to leap from my hands as instinct took over. I wrapped the blades around the attacker's feet, sending him crashing to the ground. His friends hesitated, uncertain, until my blades sliced through the air after them, seeking them like a snake. Practiced flicks of the wrist commanded my weapons, taking down the criminals until each one was unconscious and bleeding on the concrete sidewalk.

And then I glanced back. The girl stood there, frozen under the streetlight, tears streaming down her face.

Before I thought twice, I was there. "Are you okay?" I whispered, knowing she wasn't, knowing she was changed forever. Next time I'd be there to stop it.

"Where's your home?" I walked her to her apartment, waiting outside to make sure she got in safe. That's what heroes did.

As my blades wrapped around two streetlights, as I slingshot-ted myself into the sky, I made one final promise to myself.

Be the hero.

3

Normalvillains

Hope is worthless if you can't control your own destiny.

I'd spent my life watching others fall. Optimism, which seemed so great a strength, betrayed them, sent them crashing to the dirt. Painful screams filled the air as their own self backstabbed them. I promised myself I would never experience that.

What made them fall? I studied each one of my friends, then expanded my stories to the ones who didn't. The ones who succeeded. The ones who made it. History was full of their stories; they were the only ones worth remembering.

I wanted to be remembered.

The heroes were gifted with incredible power, and yet they fell too. Deaths and whispered stories of pain followed every superteam. Every mission carried a threat of more suffering.

The greatest heroes were categorized as villains. They made it. Everything they wanted was in their hands, and they never lost unless they wanted to. Supervillains, they called them—those who used their powers to go against the status quo.

The powerless had an interesting sort of power too, though.

I'd seen many rise up, seize control of their own destiny in powerful, inspiring ways. The determination to look a man in the eyes and whisper threats under your breath. The willpower to ignore the pleas for help that would only drag you back down with them.

Kings and queens who held onto their rule with vicious control often outlasted the villains who lashed out with insane schemes. The quiet menaces among us survived because they weren't an obvious threat. Their normalcy became their greatest strength. Effective invisibility could beat any superpower; they couldn't kill you if they never knew you existed. Normalvillains, then, had a power in themselves that the heroes didn't. Because something gave them that awe-inspiring drive, didn't it?

Maybe without powers, normalvillains developed a stubborn grip, a determination that if they weren't going to get supernatural help, then they'd make sure they would never need it. They'd succeed for themselves. Maybe without powers, normalvillains defined themselves, forging their own paths. Their strength was forged through flame, not given through circumstance. Their power came from their unyielding spirit, that hope that they found for themselves.

Not a hope in outside circumstances. But a kind of hope that you would do anything for.

Normalvillains would do anything for hope. The heroes were no different.

Except that they *failed*.

The one who would sacrifice their loved ones was infinitely stronger than the one who would kneel for a stranger. Someone who would cause others suffering to get ahead was almost above humanity, beyond weakness.

That ruthlessness. That defined the successful.

9

Maybe they weren't heroes. But maybe I didn't want to be. Because heroes fell. But villains? Never.

4

Cursed

Powers were a curse.

I stared at my hands, watching the ink race through my veins. Black as night, constantly flowing. It gave me the ability to write the story. The world echoed my wishes. Buildings redesigned themselves to accommodate me. Storms split to avoid soaking me.

The only thing I could never control was the people.

And how I wanted to.

The moment I'd gotten my abilities, the *moment* someone had found out—everything had crashed. The life I'd built. The life I'd wanted.

All given away in exchange for responsibility I never asked for and had no hope of carrying.

I floated into the air silently, watching the city as it slept. Even now, they expected me to work. Not sleep. Not relax. Sacrifice.

A hero or a villain. Those were your choices if you had powers.

And you were judged either way.

I clenched my fists, wrapping the red cape that followed me around one hand. Then, shutting my eyes momentarily, I ripped it away and let it fall slowly to the street below.

This wasn't fair.

I'm not a hero! I wanted to scream. All of humanity existed in the in-between—why couldn't I? If I wasn't using my powers to protect, I was failing. If I used them and still lost, I was a menace. If I used them in a way the public disagreed with, I was a demon.

I wish I'd never had them.

I felt the powers tugging at me, but I wasn't strong enough to change something so fundamental. I could change so many things, but nothing to help me now. Nothing could help me now.

My powers hated me. I was hated because of them.

5

Nighthawk

They called her the Nighthawk.

A huntress. An assassin.

She was the most dangerous type of villain. A criminal, forced to hone her skills through trial and struggle, only to stumble upon abilities to push her to another level.

We were ready.

They called her a god. The Queen of Kills. The Stealth Serpent.

One of my men collapsed behind me, his silenced words the only sign of his death. It was a warning. She wouldn't be so stupid as to attack one who was actively conversing again. The next time she struck, we'd be unaware.

I lit a torch, ignoring my heart thudding inside my chest as the beat grew louder and louder. It felt like the noise left my body, continuing the same beat in my ears, in the room, until I realized it had. She'd echoed my heartbeat through her stronghold.

How?

I couldn't hear my heart anymore. But I could feel it. And it still echoed around me. A reminder of why I was scared. And a reminder that she hunted fear.

Why did we do this? I swore silently under my breath, clenching my fists tightly around my blade. I was the strongest hero of my generation. The obvious choice to challenge the Nighthawk.

And I was here, scared.

Closing my eyes tightly, I tugged at my heartstrings, at the invisible cords that tied me to the world. With a crack, the statue hidden in the mist crumbled, and shards of rock tumbled to the ground. Raising my hand in the air, I commanded them, and the shards raced around me in a careful loop of commanded gravity. I reversed the force in a small field around myself, lifting into the air as I waited for her next move. The rocks spun around me faster and faster, effectively working as a deadly barrier.

Thud. Another man gone. My pulse shot up, and instinctively, I fired another stone into the darkness. It thudded against the ground, then everything went eerily silent. The beat was gone. I couldn't hear anyone.

The Silencing.

Suddenly, the last of my crew I could see was lying on the ground, dead or unconscious, I wasn't sure.

Spinning, I dropped gravity rapidly around me, sending anyone around me crashing to the ground. Not a glimpse of her.

A single feather drifted down through the air in front of me. Hauntingly slow. Black as if it had been dipped in ink.

A knife split through my side. The rocks fell to the earth silently.

"Leave me alone," the Nighthawk growled. "Just stop this."

Then, quieter. "You should've run while you could, Cora."

She stalked off, leaving me bleeding out on her soft rug. Even as my vision wavered and my ties to the earth grew faint, I tugged at gravity, expecting a response. But nothing happened.

14

I wasn't a superhero anymore. I was just dying.
I should've known some foes weren't worth challenging.

6

This Time

The rubble shifted, somehow weighing down even more heavily on top of me, shoving me deeper into the dirt, into the earth. Into failure.

I refused to fail.

I bit my tongue, and the sharp tang of blood anchored me for a moment. Couldn't slip away. There were still people under here.

"Go!" I shouted, feeling the power slipping away. Feeling the other power slipping in. Taking over. *No.* Wait.

A little girl looked up at me, eyes betraying a shattered heart, as she tugged at her mother's hand under the rubble. "Help Mama," she begged. "Please.'

Please.

Memories rippled loose, like ropes had been severed. Every other time I'd heard that word and failed. Every loss that I'd buried.

Another little girl, just like this one.

A young man, maybe sixteen, clutching his girlfriend's hand.

An old man, with the reflections of his burning home in his

eyes.

So many things I'd failed to save.

The pain changed me. But I couldn't let it take me.

This one will be different.

It had to be. How was I supposed to take more suffering?

Every single day was a compromise, bartered failures and losses, weighed against the victory that cost so much.

Not this time.

My hand shook with exertion, every vein popping as the effort burned through my body, and yet I moved my other hand off, used my last shred of power, disintegrated the rocks holding her mom captive.

The rocks above me crumbled, forcing my onto my knees. The weight rested on my back, just barely above the little girl. Tears streamed down my face as I trembled, every thought ripped away and replaced with pain.

One more thought. I let go, grabbed the girl and her mom. Time felt slow, maybe like God gave time for my actions, bent the rules for this final moment. I dove, leaving them outside the rubble as it collapsed, smashing into me with an explosion of dust and raw power that sent everything flying backwards.

Everything except me, because I was gone.

7

Quiet

"Quiet!"

The word was spoken with such tired, forceful *power*, that it rippled through the air and stole the words. Every head in the room turned. Who dared to shush the Council of Heroes?

I did.

"Sela," one of the women whispered, but it felt more like an accusation, a chastisement. I didn't care.

"You all are stupid." My fist clenched tightly against my side, gripping the fabric of my supersuit tightly. "This path will lead to casualties in the hundreds."

"We know what we're doing," Captain Dash shot back, annoyance lacing his voice, and discussion erupted once more.

I was ignored once more.

Something snapped. Absolutely. Not.

"I SAID QUIET!" This time, the words acted for themselves. With fire in my eyes, I ripped away the voices of everyone in attendance. The entire town square fell silent. The wind stopped. The cameras and audio went dark. "Listen."

"I'm tired of being quiet. I'm tired of standing by while

18

everyone dies." Everyone's eyes were on me. Finally. "I'm the youngest among you. But you all? You're idiots." It felt vindicating to get to say that, and a small grin spread across my face.

The entire city was quiet. Forced to listen.

My powers had been ignored for far too long. This was a long time coming.

"I respected you when you ignored me." My voice was sharp, full of malice. "I stayed quiet, because I wanted to earn a spot here. Because I thought you were smarter. But ignoring me? That's the stupidest thing you could've done." I locked eyes with the Captain. "I've always had this power. You just silenced it.

"You all choose your acts of glory and epic battles over this city. Every fight you encounter ends up here, where a million reporters can record it, where every civilian has to deal with the buildings you destroyed and the lives you stole along the way. Half of you are just as guilty as any villain. You're vain, attention-seeking failures."

Everyone was quiet. I wasn't sure if that was my powers or not.

"And if you don't fix it soon, it'll be too late."

8

Songheroes

Lightning. It struck around the battlefield.

Thunder. It echoed in their hearts.

The team stood, weapons at the ready, preparing mentally to give their lives. The monsters would be here any moment. But we were heroes. We could do this.

I readied my abilities, reaching into each of my teammates' minds to connect my power. Our bonds, strengthened by countless hours of practice, whispered their songs through the air that only I could hear as we prepared to fight nature itself.

Jake. The smart-aleck I'd hated at first, with his quick wit and insane confidence. His gun rested on his shoulder, and I could hear a small sigh in his mind. A preparation. I watched him carefully as his fist clenched, the strength surging to life throughout his body. Purple light raced down his veins towards his hand. He was ready.

His song whispered of confidence shielding a layer of concern. Not for himself—he was prepared to sacrifice if need be. Slain friends called out as soft echoes in his song, weaved through the melody like a haunting flute. As I listened, I could picture the team's bodies on the ground, the wicked smile on the faces of the monsters as they celebrated their victory. A loud drumbeat shot into the rhythm, determined to wipe the slate. The image shifted—I watched him diving into the horde, using his last ounce of strength to drive them away from the team. I watched myself under attack, sharp red fangs reaching towards my neck, just before he threw himself in the way and collapsed at my feet, the strength fading from his eyes.

I shook my head. "That's not happening," I promised softly to his song, hoping the reassurance would echo back to his own mind. I hummed, sending back notes of strength, confidence, and affection. He stiffened, and I heard his song shift slightly, the tempo increasing as the energy flowed into him.

Sadie. Her rebellious-looking blue hair hid the sweet caring girl underneath, but she'd been hurt so many times before that it was buried deep. She fought for a family—I could hear the notes of acoustic in her electric guitar melody. She tried to bury it under notes of hardened warrior, violent assassin, and lethal threat, but the softer chords reminded me of the smile I'd seen her show when she held her toddlers to her chest. The slight smile of contentment that sometimes made it out when the whole team was together, sharing a pizza and laughing. The smile when her husband's arm was around her shoulders, holding her tight. I heard him promising that it'd be okay no matter what. They'd get through this. She was incredible. And even though he had no idea what superheroing was like, I could tell she believed him.

I couldn't stop the grin that played on my lips as I quietly sang the words I knew would get through. She couldn't hear, didn't know I was listening, but she reacted all the same. I focused on reminding her of the moments we shared, of the reason she took up the fight. We could do this—we had to.

I stood in the middle of the circle as lightning crashed down around us and the world exploded. The dirt shot up around our circle, revealing beasts that were meant to stay hidden. Nature's guardians.

A sharp claw sliced into Liam's chest. I watched him clutch it, watched his step falter, heard the music stop for a second. Blood slid down his suit as a drum and piano clashed. His song screamed of pain, suffering, and a desire to stop it all. I heard him struggle, knowing he could stop it in a second. Green electricity danced around his neck, covering his body in a split-second emerald outline. But he wouldn't. He would fight through the pain, because he loved the team he was fighting for. He loved the team he fought for. And the power that he released would destroy everything nearby.

I bit my lip, sending a few notes of my own song to intermingle with his. My powers intermingled with his, turning the outline teal as blue electricity stitched his wound together. Soft, reassuring piano told him that there was a break in the pain, that if he kept fighting, he'd be okay, and we'd be safe. I dulled his pain with notes of a flute. The steady beat of a drum reminded him that we had this covered, that we were going to be victorious.

As I felt the notes flow out of me, the song leave my body and merge with his, I felt a little weaker, felt a shot of his pain. I shook my head. This was my job. I took the pain, mended the broken.

An angry beast crashed into the ground beside me, leaving an indent in the hard, cracked ground. Mia. White and golden armor covered the knight-like figure as she roared, revealing sharp, bloodstained teeth. As she swept her arm across the battlefield, the echoes off of it rippled through the air, tearing through armor and slamming enemies back with pure force. Without a tap, she could send a foe across a battlefield. Her eyes lit up with inhuman hunger as she charged, leaping through the air to slam a massive blade into the ground. The echoes around it split the earth, sending monsters screaming and falling in a circle around her.

I'd known Mia long enough to expect the quiet notes that flowed through her song. When I'd first attempted to bond with her, I'd planned for the strongest notes I'd ever heard. I prepared my mind for the onslaught of heavy metal music that I was sure was coming. Instead, I saw hints of a broken girl, full of fierce love for her city and her world. When she calmed down and returned to the preteen girl, I'd met a kid who loved serving. Every day spent in a homeless shelter or soup kitchen felt just as good to her as the night she would spend patrolling the streets. Fierce love defined her, and it echoed in a guitar's melody.

Humming slightly, I added to her song, reminding her of all the people that watched from the screens, the families whose lives depended on our victory here. I reminded her of our team and their determination. Strength shot through her song like a bullet when I added notes of determination and drums. I healed a wound with the gentle breeze of a guitar, mending her arm with soft, baby blue.

I floated in the midst of the battle as songs echoed around me. Invisible sounds that danced through the air, revealing the true hearts of my comrades. I could see what powered them through what powered me.

The true reason they all fought was what I had to address when I reached out to each mind. Echoing their deepest desires allowed me access, allowed me to strengthen and heal. I had to know them. I had to love them.

Because love drives every hero.

9

Mistakes

The silence screamed in my head, echoing until it drowned out every other thought, every other notion.

It left only pain.

My fist collided with the earth, leaving cracks in the pavement. A mistake. Another one.

Why couldn't I stop making mistakes?

My chest heaved, my eyes blurred with tears that had already been cried. My spirit burned, my morals held to the flame.

Keep going, they told me. *Heroes push through.*

But how could it hurt so much? How could it be worth it to feel this pain?

She was *dead*. Because I thought myself a hero.

"I thought you'd save her," the villain had sneered as he held Bailey over the edge. Over the cliff.

I can't fly. I remembered that thought, hitting me like a freight train. I'd been able to achieve similar feats before, but only if I could push off. An extended leap.

There was nothing to land on. I would die.

I locked eyes with her, and knew she was already dead.

And then the villain was.

It was a blur, watching her fall, and then acting with the quiet confidence of a man who just watched his wife die. There wasn't time for grief, for pain, not then. There was time for revenge.

Then I'd slaughtered the entire team of villains. Wiped their accomplices from the earth. Ripped apart a mob base with my bare hands.

And now I stood here, hands shaking.

I just wanted to hold her one more time.

This pain was impossible. And if this was heroism, I didn't want it.

10

King

He watched from the balcony, feeling the purpose settle in his heart. This was needed. This was his time.

And then he leapt.

The king plummeted from the edge of his palace, spinning through the air with a grace unmatched by any bard, then crashed into the street. His fist struck the pavement, and power rippled out—power that he didn't remember he had. Power that could rip apart.

Fear.

Even as he felt it well up inside of himself, he formed it into a whip, glowing with purple violence.

You'll die.

Leave them without a king.

Fail here, and you're worthless. Everything you've done is pointless.

You've never used these powers. How will you beat an army?

Instead of listening, he glanced to the skies, offering a counter-narrative through his thoughts. A prayer that called on the strength of a higher King, instead of his.

Fear is a liar.

The man's shield crumpled as the king's weapon morphed into an axe. Then, as the ruler spun, ice-blue power of love shot out, wrapping around his blade and forming a shield. He raised it just in time, watching it forge as another soldier's blade sliced downwards, only to meet unstoppable steel.

Protect them.

Like a dancer he weaved in and out of the combat, duelling four opponents at a time, moving on in the span of a second. His weapon flashed between emotions and tools like a flickering flame, taking different shapes each time.

It feels so good, he thought, letting the hint of a smile spread over his face. This power he'd locked away, hidden for a day that he'd hoped would never come. The role of a king wasn't to fight, but to protect, to uplift lives.

He couldn't uplift lives if there were none left, so this seemed necessary.

Who are you?

The voice felt foreign, and it shocked him still halfway through an attack. A shortsword cut into his armor, and he felt the impact even as he snapped back to reality. Red anger accentuated his kick as he swung his body through the air, making solid connection with the enemy's head. The warrior crumpled, and the king yanked out the blade, tossing it to the side as a bloody reminder.

Who are you? it asked again, but this time he kept fighting, refused to listen.

I'm a king. A hero, he reminded himself. *A hero.*

It continued to shout, the voice growing louder each time. Each shout was another bolt of pain and confusion, another weight slowing him down.

Who. Are. You.

He shut his eyes, forcing himself with a will that no man could rival to keep going.

It doesn't matter, he responded, feeling his confidence grow with each syllable. *Because this life isn't mine.*

11

Mortal

Shredding pain didn't just threaten to rip me apart; it actively did. Even as every cell felt like it was being stabbed, ripped apart, sliced into pieces, I clung onto life like a spark of fire in a rainstorm. As everything pounded down, as I lost my mind, as I couldn't think, I knew it would be okay. This pain would pass.

And when I went to stop it, nothing happened.

My hand stayed there for a moment, raised in the gesture that had summoned shields before. The glowing green power that strengthened me, conformed to my will, healed my allies, was gone. Like it was never there in the first place.

Blinking through pain, I tried again, pouring everything I had into the gesture, begging it to work, and *nothing.*

It hurt worse.

Destructive.

Who even was I?

I felt myself grow weaker as the energy roared through me, the black power of decay eating at my body as everything burned. I felt the mortal that I'd forgotten about return, felt the weakness that defined me before, felt *pain.*

Pain, unlike anything else. Pain like grief.

I was dead.

The next week, two, three, were misery. My team had rescued me, but they'd lost me. I wasn't alive anymore. It was someone else. An ordinary person.

I'd watch my team fight monsters, watch them struggle. I watched people die, and I had to stand by, unable to help.

I was no longer a hero. I was powerless.

Somehow, I ended up here every night. The same routine, so much I should be unfazed by now; shaking sobs, my chest feeling like it'll snap, and my head feeling like I deserved to die, or maybe like I barely deserved to live.

Pain.

Mortality. That was the worst part.

The instinct that I'd honed, deflecting the most minuscule of scrapes or cuts with sage green power, was useless now. I'd make the motions, follow through, and it would fail, and I'd have to go look up how to handle a cut. A cut. I was reduced to that.

The bandage fell off and hit the ground below me as I sobbed, staring out into the waves, begging my reflection to save me. I locked eyes with the other me; the rippling water separated us, and it felt just like my spirit. Divided between me before and after. My identity ripped away, my old self dead. And I missed it so much.

Godhood. I'd never said it aloud. But I was powerful. And now that had been stripped away.

It hurt more than losing my parents.

Now, every death after was because I wasn't there.

The moon moved behind a cloud, and it went dark.

I wish I was a hero, I whispered to myself as a golden line streaked across the sky.

Until it crashed down next to me.

A golden figure crashed into the earth. The concrete was destroyed in a pit forty feet wide and thirty feet deep. A woman's body rested in the center. Burn marks were evident. Blood covered her casual clothing.

Without even thinking, I'd slid down the pit, moved towards the body. She had a pulse.

Blue.

A sudden blur of ice cold blue, slamming me to the side of the pit. My back hit the crumbling concrete, and pain flared up in my spine. I groaned, clutching my back as I tried to force myself back to my feet, stumbling slightly.

Another woman stood there. Blue as an ice sculpture, and with all the expression of one too. A twisted crown of flowing water wrapped around her skull. Sharp, elegant cheekbones, pristine makeup, and the regal expression of a spoiled child told me she thought too much of herself.

The girl from before. The golden crash survivor.

She looked ordinary.

Still unconscious, she waited in the center. Pain was inevitable, and the ice woman knew this. She took calculated steps, eying her prey like a lion.

Until, suddenly, I tackled her.

A grin split my face as we both wrestled in the air. The sidewalk seemed further and further away as we slammed down at terminal velocity, destined to meet the water far below at any second. Destined to meet death.

I was okay with that, though.

"*A hero,*" I whispered.

12

Heroes 1.0

"We have to."

The Council was silent. The Vanguards ceased their arguing. And they listened to me.

A final meeting. Emergency call. The sirens had echoed through the streets, alerting every hero that we needed them. I needed them.

I was a human. But I needed the strong to survive.

"We caused this," I repeated, the same thing I'd been saying for an hour. "This is our fault. So it's up to us to end it."

"Soar." Will's voice was steady, but I could sense the wavering doubt. "Soar, we'll die."

I met his eyes, and nodded. A faint smile. "I know."

Purpose. That driving force. Crystalized in this moment.

I knew how it would end. But I knew it was how it had to.

Wrapping my hand around my blades on the table, I stood. The window stayed open during meetings; an emergency escape, in case of ambush. Now, I needed to get out. I'd let them come up with their ideas.

I wanted to be with my city while I still could.

My blades wrapped around the pole sitting just outside the window, and I yanked on the chain. With a running start, I launched into the sky.

I felt like a legend.

I spiraled downwards like it was second nature, like an eagle, before swinging out of my fall with a carefully-placed scythe. My blades danced and sang as I wrapped the chain around a mugger, who was sprinting away from an angry woman with her shoe in her hand. Quietly he collapsed to the ground. When I handed the woman the bag, the look of relief on her face was like I had just solved all her problems.

This is what I lived for.

I flung myself back into the skies, soaring like an eagle. The bird spread across my chest, taking off in flight, frozen in gold across my blue suit. The gold cloak followed me through the air, emphasizing my silhouette against the sky. It would hide me, make me invisible when I needed it.

Home. I had to stop. Had to make sure James was okay.

"Hey, bro!" I called as I swung the door open, stepping into our house in my civilian clothes. He knew, of course, but it wasn't worth convincing the press that Soar had a habit of walking into random houses that weren't mine.

"Paul!" James stepped out of his bedroom, closing the door softly behind him. At his side, he held a thin laptop. In his ears were earbuds, probably pulsing with a beat that was silent to me.

"How was school?" We sat down on the couch, each assuming our normal spots. It was something different from every other sibling pair. We weren't enemies. We were allies. And he was my hero.

He shrugged. "Same as every day. Heroing?"

I shrugged. "Emergency meeting. I'm sure you heard. Those are boring though, so I left early." I half-grinned, and he burst into laughter.

"You just left a Council emergency meeting?" He shook his head. "Legendary."

"Yeah." I leaned back, snagging a can of soda that had been left on the counter. "I should probably head back out. They'll need me, y'know. Since I'm so cool."

He went kind of quiet for a moment. "I think you hold the city together more than you know."

I forced a smile. "Yeah, maybe. Doubt it. I'm powerless." I stood, stretching. "You want dinner?"

"Yeah. I'll start it if you want to go hero again." He stood up too. "Pizza good?"

I laughed. "Your specialty."

While he started cooking, I left for my room, shutting the door behind me and quietly locking it. Alone.

My chest shook. My hand trembled.

I wouldn't survive this. I knew it already.

It was a bigger threat than anything else we'd faced. And it was our fault. A dragon, forged of legends, come to feast on our powers. And it would eat everything in its wake. Its roar echoed across galaxies. Its claws could split a city down the middle. The penetrating gaze could freeze a man.

Both of my hands were shaking as I pulled out my chair, sitting at my desk. A box rested by my feet. I reached for it, pulled it out, and opened it. They were still there. My gift.

A piece of paper to my left. A pen. I snagged both. I had to write something.

I sat there for half an hour, pouring my heart and thoughts into the paper, until James called for dinner. Finishing up my letter, I slid it into the box, then quickly sketched an eagle on top and signed my brother's name. *I need to get this somewhere safe.*

After dinner, I picked up the scythes again. Time to leave. To help my city.

One final warning to James, just like always.

"Be the hero," I told him, winking just like always.

And then I stepped out into the night.

The sirens had gone silent. But the city was still waiting. I fingered the edge of my cloak. A cape now, really, after the fight last night. I hated capes. Hopefully I had time to fix mine.

We didn't know when the beast would come. And that almost made it worse.

"Glide," I heard a woman's soft voice whisper. Then, louder, "Hey." Sela landed on the rooftop besides me. A level of careful, controlled power hovered around her like a tangible aura. Each word she spoke had the potential for power.

She wasn't loud. But that was okay. We sat there on the rooftop that I didn't realize I'd stopped on. Watched the moon rise slowly into the skies. I traced each star, hoping they would carry my legacy too. Hoping I would be remembered.

"I don't want to die," I admitted. Quietly.

She nodded, still gazing at the stars, but I knew she understood. "None of us do. But we have to."

"Sacrifice." I sighed. "Purest form of heroism, I suppose. Go out with a bang. Isn't that what we all want?"

She shrugged. A kind of quiet wisdom lined her steady breaths. It was something people never seemed to notice, because she hung at the back of the crew. She was still so young. Fifteen. She didn't deserve to die. Not now.

"Now what?" she asked, and I felt my questions echoed in the tremor of her voice. "Do we just... wait?"

"I guess we have to."

The next morning, we reconvened at the Council building. I stepped into the room, this time carrying the confidence of someone who knew how it would end, and set down my box. "Whoever survives?" I caught the eyes of everyone on the team. They all glanced away uncomfortably. I wasn't sure if they were scared of dying or living alone. "Someone." I met Will's eyes. "Someone needs to get this to James."

He nodded, almost imperceptibly.

"When that beast arrives, we'll enter war like we've never seen." My words carried power. I was their leader without a vote. Because I was still human. They trusted me.

"When that beast arrives," I continued, "we'll fight like demons. And we'll fight to the death. It comes for legends. For power. For stories. The only way to stop it is to conclude ours."

A caught breath. Then, a woman, dressed in all blue—Psycha—asked, "You mean sacrifice?"

I nodded gravely. "It's our only option. We're the Vanguards. We protect the people." I met everyone's eyes. "Even if it takes everything."

Will's finger burst into flames. A nervous habit; heat calmed him. I swallowed, pushing down my own fears. But my left hand played with a scythe I wasn't holding, twisting the weapons that had become so second nature that I was acting without them.

A golden woman, eyes glowing with determination, stepped forward. "We have to," she agreed. "We're mortal. We're superheroes. We should be the best of them. And any of them would die for us." Her left cheek was scarred, her arms carried burn marks, but she stood stronger than most of the people around her.

When the beast arrived, I was at lunch with James. I caught his eye one last time. Wishing our parents would take care of him, but knowing they wouldn't.

"James."

He looked up, fork frozen mid-air. "What?"

"Thank you." I swallowed. "For being the hero. For being my hero."

As I shut the door, pulling my mask on and using my camouflage to vanish into the noon light, I called out one more time: "James. Always be the hero."

It was a promise to him, even if I didn't say it. I would be the hero. For him.

My tattered cape trailed behind me as I raced into the skies, traveling at lightspeed through the streets above the city. The beast was formed of old ruins, something that looked like a temple, with a golden helmet and shards of statue gold and stone intertwined. A dragon that hovered, glowing with otherworldly powers. Crackling with lightning. Spikes of racing water lined its back. Teeth of sharp daggers lined its mouth.

"Are you all ready?" It was a stupid question, and I knew that when I asked it. Who was ready to die?

Except I was.

My scythe raced through the air above the city as I blinked in and out of sight. Danced in and out of sight like a ghost. I landed a deep cut into the stone of the dragon's eye, slicing down to the golden shield that filled its left eyesocket.

I swung down to land, softly hitting the concrete besides the grounded members of my team. Every hero was here today. Everyone was ready for this. We had to be.

A collective gasp filled the air as every hero watched the cut I made reverse. The dragon roared louder than before and swept a claw at me. In an instant, I had vanished, camouflaging myself and flinging my body into the air.

"Bow." Sela's voice crackled with raw power. She glowed white as she hovered in the air, her fingers shaking at her side.

The beast stumbled, one knee collapsing, then surged to its feet. A claw sent her crashing to a wall, which crumbled around her. I heard a shout, a dome of white, and the building collapsed in a puff of dust.

King—that was what we all called him, even though we weren't his subjects—leapt into the fray with a glowing axe, splitting the neck of the beast even as Sela erupted out of the rubble. I reappeared, digging a blade into its arm and another into its head, hanging between the chains as I pulled downwards. My blades slid inwards, cutting deeper with every second.

Captain Dash was in and out before I even noticed, scaling the beast's body and slamming a spear into its head. He flipped off the skull, landing in front of it, and then shook so violently the earth shook with him. His body blurred, surround in echoes of himself as the concrete cracked and the beast stumbled.

"We're close!" I screamed, loosening one blade to pull myself up and dig into a new spot. Down its spine, interrupting the water, then it its belly, stabbing into a grey piece of stone.

In the blink of an eye, Captain Dash was dead, his body pierced through with a bloody claw. I yanked hard on both of my blades as the beast turned towards me, then pulled myself out of the way and vanished again.

Instead, it hit the King, sweeping him through the air. He soared across the skies, guaranteed to land at a speed at a rate that no one could survive.

"Die." I'd never heard Sela so full of hatred. Everything froze. An internal battle raged—her iron will against the beast's sheer power. It began to shrivel, to fall apart.

Then it roared, and she just… vanished.

She just vanished.

Its breath stole her from existence, inhaled her into its legends, but I heard her scream one more command.

"REGRET!" echoed through the air a moment before her sacrifice lit up bright white, filling the dragon from the inside, and it collapsed to the ground, shrieking in pain.

I raced forward, slicing a blade into the mouth, another into an eye, then again into a leg, and another, systematically leaving cuts all over it, killing it slowly. The golden woman took one leg, her blade dancing, followed by slices of ice that split into the dragon's body and drove it apart.

I'm a human, I reminded myself as I watched her die, as I watched her smash into a crumbling building, recorded on live TV. *I'm supposed to hurt. This keeps me strong.*

But it hurt watching everyone die.

Unlike anything else. It hurt.

Will had been systematically burning off shards of the beast. He caught my eye from the opposite end of the battlefield as the dragon roared. Just like the King's blade, its claws shaped into a scythe to mimic mine. The water that formed its spikes wrapped into a cloak that covered its eyes.

It wanted me next.

This was its warning.

"Come and get me," I whispered, arcing back into the air.

Yanking myself back and forth in the air, I challenged the dragon, blades slicing into it again and again as its imitations only hit empty air. Will hovered behind it, flames shooting out from his palms and burning it alive, shattering its stone as I battled it in the air. I hovered like a god, restrained by human

40

ability, pulling myself up again relentlessly in a fight against gravity. But I wouldn't die.

Not yet.

I would. But it would matter.

And I would make this beast feel my pain first.

Below, I heard war cries. I spared half an instant to look. Civilians were gathering below, with butcher knives and antique blades and guns that hadn't been touched in years, with frying pans and forks. With a sense of purpose and good.

And they fought for their lives.

As we destroyed the beast from above, they fought from below, slicing off one leg effectively, causing its scream to ripple and shatter the highest floors of buildings.

It sliced out at me with its normal claw, cutting into my face, leaving trails of blood, but I yanked myself towards it and dug my feet into its eyes and cut into its face. *You'll regret that*, I promised it.

Finally, enraged, the beast grew five times in size, towering over anything I could imagine. Determined, I pulled myself up to its maw one more time, before falling.

I knew what was about to happen.

As the beast swung its scythe towards the city, seconds away from slicing into *my* city, *my* people, I wrapped my blades around it, yanked, heard them snap, but it slowed it, then I fell, spiraling into the path and taking the hit for them.

"Be the hero."

For my people.

For my city.

I watched Will watch me, watch me fall, and watched his flames ripple with rage.

And then the blade hit.

And it all went dark.

13

Aliveheroes

Power like a soft flame on a breath of smoke, begging for release, for destruction. It roared inside of me, a reminder of what could be.

And it was time to let it be.

I locked eyes with the beast, forcing myself back to my feet. I needed energy, so I allowed the flame to race through my veins for a moment, wincing at the burn. The bodies of my friends, barely hanging onto life, some already lost, lay around me.

I was the last of the Vanguards. They'd all fallen doing what they loved. Protecting.

But it wasn't enough. They'd all failed, hadn't they? The threat was still here.

I refused to stop. I couldn't. I wouldn't.

The flames shot up around my feet, burning scars deeper into my ankles as they danced around the ground. With a running leap I launched into the air.

Persevere, I thought as the flames that surrounded my body burned hotter and hotter.

Keep going, I demanded of my body as the outline of the flame etched itself deeper into my chest with the red ink of fire.

Push through the pain, I reminded myself as the fire ripped at my skin, sending burnt pieces of my hair into the air behind me. I was fire-resistant, but nothing was fire-proof. Not to this flame. It tore me apart, ripped to the base of my humanity.

But as I spared one last glance at the city behind me, I knew it was worth it. I would be a hero.

A flying fist packed the strength of the sun as a blast shot me crashing back down to earth. Dirt flew threw the air as I smashed into the ground, sliding backwards.

It hurts.

Push through.

That's what heroes did.

I watched the beast stumble. The monster, with purple horns that shifted in the smoke, a black demon formed of the fears and shadows of mankind. The mythological figures that haunted nightmares, forged together. A scythe in its left hand, a hood over its face, bloody fangs waiting for a bite.

And yet it stumbled as the fire rippled out from my impact. It shook, nearly about to fall, before the shadows of the world around raced upwards and strengthened it. Lines of black raced through the air, weaving together to repair the beast's wounds.

I could do this.

Another attack. Another crash into the hard dirt. My body screamed for relief, but I gave a bit more to the flame, looked up at the beast with hard, determined eyes, and stood back up.

I won't stop.

The flames grew even hotter. The fire inside me was its own beast. Its own monster.

And I planned to release it.

I grew in size as I raced across the ground, blazes fueling my every step. Red, then orange, then yellow, then white, white so hot it threatened to tear me to ashes, then blue, the blue of a star, of an ungodly heat, then purple as I got closer. The limits of my power, they said. The limits.

Limits were made to break.

Half a second before I launched through the air, it grew hotter. I felt a scream being ripped out of my soul itself through inhuman pain as a monster–sized version of myself, surrounded by purple flames, watched the color fade. Invisible flame. The hottest flame.

My memory began to burn like the pages of a book.

Time froze as I reached out, begging for it to stop for a moment.

Willy? My little sister, holding a candle, eyes bright with joy as she waited. *Can you light this?* When I did, she whispered, *That's so cool.*

My first heroic moment.

William, my girlfriend whispered, lying in the dirt.

The first one I couldn't save.

William, she repeated. She'd repeated my name like a plea for help. Like she needed me. And that hurt more than any flame.

Will, never give up.

The chorus of voices in my mind echoed through my soul. My mother, my grandfather, my team. My girl.

I won't give up. For you, I promised. *For you.*

I clenched my eyes tight as the flames brought me back, as they burnt those memories too. As they destroyed everything about me.

They could never destroy me.

My eyes lit with an inhuman flame or an inhuman stubborn-ness. One of the two.

Either way, it was what I needed.
They'd tried to limit me. Then they'd lost.
I had no limits. And I never lost.
I persevere.
Because I'm a hero.

14

Rise

Sacrificing is stupid.

I decided that as I knelt, numb, with the cape in my hands. Burnt fabric was all I had left of my brother. The guy who had raised me, kept me safe, kept me fed when our parents forgot. When I was struggling, he'd kneel down next to me, one knee up, look me in the eyes, and whisper, "You can be anything, James. Be the hero."

The hero. A role I'd fought to fill my entire life, oblivious that my brother was the expert. For a decade he'd been operating as Soar, the cloaked vigilante that danced around town, spinning through the air like a witch. Our town called him the shadow, sometimes, because the criminals did, because that was the only way we could make sense of him.

It was so quiet.

He would dance in and out of combat, swinging through the air, vanishing without a trace before reappearing over a bad guy's head. With a camouflage suit and blades on the ends of chains, he was the only non-superpowered hero in the city, but he was the most powerful. Everyone knew that Soar was the king of the city.

Everyone knew that the city would fall apart without him.

Now, his grapple blades rested, ends embedded in the dirt. Scars ran up and down their handles, markers from every fight. The miniature scythes gleamed viciously—he'd just sharpened them the night before.

"Be the hero," I whispered as I clutched his cape. Tears filled my eyes, but I blinked them away, not knowing why, but knowing exactly why, knowing that heroes couldn't afford weakness.

His cape. Such a stupid thing, really. He'd always preferred cloaks, said capes looked stupid, but when his cloak hood had been sliced off in a high-speed battle with the Blurred, he hadn't had a chance to get it repaired. This call was unexpected, but I think he knew it was coming all the same.

Soar, they called him. Paul, I called him.

It hurt me so much more than it hurt them.

When I found out his identity, a year ago to this day, I'd begged him to stop. I'd never seen such determination in his eyes, maybe even a flash of anger at the notion that he should give up.

"Heroes don't quit," he told me, voice harder than normal, sharp as his blades. "Even when it hurts, or when it's impossible—heroes don't quit."

Last night, we sat alone at the dinner table, abandoned by our parents for yet another tour, another month's rent spent on concerts. The third time this year, and it was only February.

"Be the hero," I'd heard him whisper as he sharpened his blade absently, setting his bowl to the side.

"Paul?" I remembered my voice cracking, remembered my embarrassment, but that seemed stupid now. "Paul, you'll be okay, right?"

When he met my eyes, I saw ghosts.

"I'll be the hero," he told me simply, and went back to sharpening.

The next day, when I saw the threat arrive, my heart stopped. The team flew out to meet them. The Vanguards. They could stop anything.

Anything, I repeated internally.

I'd watched him fall.

Watched him crash.

Watched his chains snap.

He'd thrown himself in the way of the hit, deflected the attack that would've leveled the city. I'd almost felt the raw determination in the air. His voice echoed through the TV as I stared out the window. His words seemed to connect with nothing in my empty mind, as everything went dark, as my life seemed to end too.

"Be the hero," he rasped, face bloody, tears streaming down his face from the pain, before he whipped one last blade around the monster's hand and let himself fall.

The monster crashed to the ground, and it all went silent.

Or maybe it didn't, and it was just me, or maybe it did.

Maybe.

Nothing was certain.

He was dead.

How was he dead?

When I got home that day, there was a package on my doorstep, scarred with burn marks in the shapes of handprints. My name across the top, in my brother's handwriting. *James.* It felt like no one had called me that in decades, but that was just because he was dead. The last person who cared was gone, so what did I matter anyways?

The box was the length of my forearm, tied up with a black bow. I lifted the lid, letting it drop to the ground beside me.

A note.

And blades.

Grapple blades, just like his. Except his were blue. These were scarlet.

My favorite color. Now a color of pain.

The note. One more thing. A final reminder of him to hang on to. I almost didn't want to read it, because once I did, he'd have nothing more to say, and then maybe he'd really be gone.

James.

If you're reading this, the worst happened. But it's okay. I planned for this. I went out a hero, didn't I?

The city will need you. You'll need me. I'm sorry. But this is your time. You can't rise to the sun if you're covered in my shadow.

Take the blades. Make your own identity.

Be the hero.

Rise.

Rise, like a phoenix in the ashes.

You'll need me. I'm sorry.

That wasn't good enough. "Not good enough!" I shouted, without even realizing it, just echoing my thoughts against the plaster walls. I lifted the blade, feeling the balance, and swung, embedding it in my door. "Not enough," I whispered as the chain left my hand and I fell to the ground against my wall, body shaking with tears.

Sacrifice is stupid, because there would always be more threats. I needed him still. That moment wasn't enough to make up for him leaving the rest of my life behind.

I'd be the hero, because they needed me.

But I would never fall. I'd rise.

50

15

Raven

My heartbeat echoed in the slowed time. A reminder. Life was still going on.

So I reached out and slowed it more. A standstill. A moment in time, just for myself.

And then I broke down.

There was a reason no one knew about this power. My super strength, my flight, all of those I'd revealed, carefully crafting a superhero persona to use my abilities for the world. Braylen to my friends. The Raven to my enemies.

Because every time I stopped, the raven watched me.

It was there now, silently judging from a branch across the road, beady eyes locked on as I held my head in my hands. A deep, shaky breath, wiping a tear from my eyes absently. The raven was the only other figure able to move in this time.

And that meant I was finally alone.

My mom. My sister. My dad. All gone. In a blink. And I hadn't had time to process, because no, being a hero meant perfection. It meant never breaking. It meant never stopping.

No weakness, until no one else could see.

So I kept this power to myself. The slowed time. When I used it to save a life, no one questioned how a flying man managed to squeeze in between the falling rock and the ground to snag that girl. No one asked questions about how quickly I'd rescued the survivors from that burning hotel on Main Street. No one batted an eye, as long as I was helping.

And that meant this ability was my secret.

A soft thud on my shoulder caused me to open my eyes, sighing deeply as I prepared to find someone there, instinctually expecting a hand reaching out, begging for help.

Instead, I locked eyes with the raven. Its midnight-black feathers shimmered slightly in the sun, like a mirage. It had never come this close before.

Since this time was different, I let myself do something I never did.

Cry.

The sobs racked my body as I let loose, bringing up painful memory after painful memory, unprocessed trauma that was eating away at my personal time, at this limited bubble of peace, but I couldn't stop it. It hurt too much, but I needed it.

Why? I asked God, hoping *someone* would hear my prayers. *I do so much good. Why does it have to end so bad every time?*

The raven pecked me on the shoulder, and I nodded silently. Instead of waiting for an answer, I wiped my tears with my sleeve, mentally preparing myself to reenter the world.

Really, I decided as I wiped away another tear, moved back into the same position as before.. *Really, heroism is about acting. Playing the part, even when it takes everything from you.*

Heroes are liars.

16

Stillhawk

The world should be quiet.

It wasn't an opinion I wanted; it was one I had to have.

After they took the girl away, saved her from bleeding out on my floors, I breathed a silent sigh of relief. But it wasn't enough. I spent the next three days in my cold, hard chair, shaking, rocking silently, knees held to my chest. The giant, empty hall felt small as I whispered to myself, "*I had to. I did it to survive.*"

They called me a goddess. But I was a demon born of selfishness and pain.

I hurt her because I was hurting.

I remembered how loud her heartbeat sounded. Each step of the metal armor of her soldiers that felt like a drum in my head. Remembered the feeling of my world blurring, my skin feeling wrong, the air feeling tight in my lungs. I remembered them moving, and I remembered it hurt.

They came in to hurt me. And they did.

I had to do what I did.

Just like before.

The movement streaked across my skin. People left blurry trails as they moved far too fast, far too much. Zero predictability. Only chaos. Constant movement. Constant pain.

I remembered collapsing after I got the powers. Inside the cold, dark experiment room, everything was fine. And then I stepped into the city streets.

People didn't understand. Yes, I was *powerful*—it crackled at my fingertips, rose up in my throat like words that refused to be ignored—but I was *weak*. Movement *burned* me; suddenly, silence was sacred. Heartbeats drummed in my ears, knocking me off balance. Watching someone pass made me wince in pain. Crowds felt like torture methods.

QUIET.

It felt like my pulse was shouting it. The world moved too fast. And I trembled in the corner of the room, blinking back tears.

But that wasn't me anymore.

I shook my head, fingers gripping the edge of the roof even as it cut into me.

Nighthawk.

I hadn't donned this outfit in a while.

My old burglary gear, back when it was still possible for me. Black, sleek, with feathers on my shoulders and knives in the wrists. Each feather was sharpened, available as a weapon in a moment's notice. Back then, I thought I knew what power was. I thought every time I took something, I took more power.

I couldn't have been more right.

And now I didn't want power, because I'd finally taken from myself.

I shook my head quietly as I watched the city. The lights of moving cars hurt my eyes, causing streaks across my vision. I resisted the urge to grab my arms as the goosebumps returned.

Stillness.

I shut my eyes slowly, then breathed out. In an orb around me, the noises stopped. It was still. Quiet.

I was still learning control. I never really had—I'd let my abilities control me in times of pain, when people moved too fast, when they came to kill me and hurt me again by just existing.

In the quiet, memories were all too loud—doctors with strange machines, empty promises, and a searing pain that filled my body.

The worst pain was the killings after.

I didn't mean to. I lashed out.

But that didn't fix it.

When things moved too fast, I stopped them. My hands would shake, clutched to my chest as someone yelled beside me, and then I'd get bumped, or I'd brush a wall, and *no*, it wouldn't be okay anymore.

Their hearts were still.

Eventually I retreated. Used my burglary money to buy this castle. A large, empty trap, really. I lived in the very center, experiencing life alone, knowing one more person would hurt me more than I could imagine.

Now I wanted to leave that.

Stupid.

But after watching those heroes die, I couldn't stay back anymore.

I knew the people thought of me as a goddess. And my power was immeasurable. But I hadn't helped when the Vanguards faced a world-ending threat. And I hadn't stepped in when they sacrificed themselves.

That was betrayal. Not just of them. Of humanity.

I almost let humanity die, when I could've stopped it.

I sat on the edge of the roof, my legs dangling, my old gear back on. I had to do this.

It's going to hurt.

As the air rushed by my ears and the familiar pounding in my head returned, I dove towards the people, towards the chaos, towards that itchy feeling on my arms and that tight feeling in my chest, and told myself, *I'm okay with that.*

17

Memories

The memories of the pain were the worst part.

Even when the wound was gone, the cut healed, the heartbreak stopped, I remembered. Every single ache echoed. Even the ones I hadn't felt.

The ones the others had felt. The ones that I'd inflicted. The ones I'd allowed by not being strong enough.

The people viewed me as a hero, but I was broken. I wasn't a hero. I was barely a human. I was a shell of what I was before I took the mantle.

Each death, each failure, weighed heavier than any building. Super-strength couldn't help me carry the invisible burden. Flight couldn't help me escape it.

I was trapped, being broken by the powers that were supposed to save me.

I couldn't stop—I'd be killing thousands by stepping away. I couldn't keep going—I would be killing myself by continuing.

Internally, every raw atom of strength dug from my soul. It ripped away pieces until I was unrecognizable.

The pain changed me on a daily basis. I would never be the

same.

Because I was a hero.

18

Burnt

How could you go from superhero to shadow this easily?

They called him the Burnt One.

Such an interesting story. The hero who died fighting, and yet still walked among us.

I'd been following him, watching his story, writing down his truth. The Alivehero. But he was dead.

His memories had burnt in the final blow. When he lit up like a blazing sun and sacrificed everything to take down the dragon, he'd given the last of himself. That fire had burnt his soul with his body, leaving him a shadow, marked in lines of burnt flesh and scars.

It left him dead.

But he still fought.

The first thing he did after he fought? It was eerily calm. I watched as he descended from the skies, his fires extinguishing in a single breath when he touched the ground. His black hair smoked at the tips. The scars were already forming. He stepped into the Council building across the street like it was second nature, his feet seeming to move him without conscious direction. Tucked neatly inside the door was a box, about the size of a shoebox, with the symbol of an eagle sketched across the top along with a name.

The Burned One knelt, wrapping his hands around the box, and held it against his chest like it was the most priceless artifact on the earth. Smoke rose from his hands as they made contact with the wooden box, but it quickly faded into the air.

He left the package at a door, ringing the bell and dropping it on the doorstep before rocketing off into the air in a burst of flame.

I followed him for several more days, documenting each action the shadow man made.

Honestly, it didn't make sense. The Burned One fought crime just like he would before the battle. He'd step in for the weak, taking out criminals with a detached ease, then checking on the victims without a word.

He knew nothing. He was no one. And yet? He knew heroism. He was a hero.

How was he a hero?

As I wrote his story, I hunted for an answer to my question. He wasn't full of hope. He couldn't feel emotions, at least as far as I could tell.

Maybe... maybe he just was.

I watched as the man lit with a blaze that raced along the lines in his skin, as he challenged the larger-than-life man who wielded cold like a sword, stealing people's energy and lives with the flick of his wrist. I watched as the Burned One stepped in, eyes blazing with either hatred or purpose, and destroyed him with effortless power. He didn't even know what he was doing. But he knew what was right.

He was a hero because he was.

19

Fractures

"I could make the world a better place." My voice carried through the room, speaking to no one, and yet saying some of the most important words at the same time. Words that defined me.

"I can *help* people."

My hands twisted intangible pieces of the hologram, moving around my blue model of the city. The city needed heroes. After the Fall, we had no one. I could step up.

In a flash, I'd analyzed the chances. 87% we'd have another threat to the city within the month. 42% that the city would be destroyed in three.

If I didn't step in.

I couldn't stop the grin from spreading across my face as I spun in my office chair, reaching for my other desk. "I can be helpful," I whispered excitedly, brushing a stray curl out of my face.

Calculations raced through my brain like speedsters as my hands constructed the first model of many. A drone. Small, triangle-shaped, and orange, it was outfitted with a descending platform and housed a smaller robot, this one traditionally shaped, that was designed for both combat and grabbing resources for me.

My eyes lit with pride as I held the small machine in my hands, raising it towards the fluorescent lighting, tracing the intricate, historically-based designs with my thumb. Soar, scythes spinning through the air, headed towards a dragon. Another side showed a man lit on fire, diving towards an army of beasts. A third, the city skyline, peaceful. The reason I was fighting.

A good world.

If I can do this, then I have to.

Carefully I placed the contraption on my Auto-Sculpt, a custom-made machine that would replicate the robot exactly as I'd designed it.

"Where's my notebook?" I muttered, running my hands through curly hair as I raised my hand and a hologram appeared. With a few swipes in the air, I'd pulled up a digital copy of my sketchbook, full of all of my fantastical designs. Each design was signed, not with my name, Archie, but with my identity. The Architect. Each design was impossible.

Impossible for a normal kid. But not for me.

I knew that I was special. Other kids' dreams didn't come with measurements and steps, calculations and remodelings. When their imagination cooked up stories of them becoming heroes, they didn't picture the thousands of equations that went into their suits, ensuring that every microfiber was outfitted to ensure safety.

I was different.

When Soar had approached me with the opportunity to build his new suit, one outfitted with camouflage, I'd jumped at the challenge. Instead of fading in, I built technology that allowed him to vanish with the tense of a muscle, the click of his tongue. He was invisible.

After that, I was hooked.

My notebooks were filled with redesigns of heroes, devices that could help them win, reduce casualties. And once every dozen pages there was a sketch of me. Outfitted in orange armor, wielding an energy blaster in one hand, a controller in the other, and a crazed expression on my face. A genius expression.

Ever since I'd won that competition, built that mech suit for the science fair, the city had caught on that I was special. That was why Soar asked me. Why the other students gave me a wide berth.

The city was my home. If I was special, I would be betraying them to do nothing with it.

As I twisted bolts and soldered edges, tracing lines with a glowing pencil, I watched the drones that were launching off of the Auto-Sculpt, one after the other. When I built, I pictured the people I would help. And I knew I couldn't leave them to die without me.

20

Fall

I let another one die.

Was that why the shaking wouldn't stop?

My arms felt numb, my knees were weak. I was collapsing—no, I already did, I was kneeling on cold, hard pavement, clutching the body of a little girl. She couldn't have been more than seven. Her curly blonde hair looked like a crown.

"I'm sorry," I whispered. Or I thought I did, but everything was so disorienting, so lost, so dark. Choked sobs racked my body.

Hero. The word seemed like a spit in the face of what I'd done.

Heroes were perfect. They never failed. But I only failed more and more with each passing day.

The woman last week. Died in my arms just out of the reach of the fire.

Two kids, four and nine. Building collapse. I was busy fighting.

A man, shoved his kids out first and collapsed. He was the hero when I wasn't there.

The ice only spread around me, seeping into the concrete. But my world felt like a fiery hell.

"What happened?" a loud voice asked, shoving a microphone in my face—but *no, not now*, so I shoved it away, accidentally letting a burst of ice cover it and race towards the man. He dropped it with a shriek, eyes wide as his technology covered in frozen water.

"Get away from me," I whispered, voice breaking, soul breaking.

There were so many people. So many people watched me breaking. A crowd, pushing inwards. They wanted to see their hero fall.

The ice burst, then slowed. I got to my feet, reverently setting down the girl below me. My hands shook, trembling by my side. I brushed a bang out of my face.

Must've been funny, watching a grown man fall apart, watching a hero crumble under the weight of grief no one else bore.

This girl had been left here, alone, in the midst of an attack. Her mom ran off. She was abandoned.

I shook my head as my body trembled. My hands wouldn't move; my breath felt short, quick.

"Get away from me!" I snapped, thrusting out a hand. Sharp icicles grew out of the ground, forming a barrier around me— enforced by the fear in their eyes.

You're not a hero.

"I'm trying." I clenched a fist, ran my hand through my hair, stared down at the little girl, and choked on my words. What could I say in a moment like this?

I could make the world bow with my powers. I could ensure this never happened again.

But instead I had to keep watching them fall. To do the right thing meant to let them live their lives, even if it hurt others. I had to stand back.

And that broke me.

"What happened?" they asked again, and this time, I shook my head, didn't touch the mic.

The woman with the mic spun around, facing the camera, and began rattling off lines. "A villain arc!" she proclaimed. "The fall of a hero."

I shut my eyes against the *pain*.

Then I grabbed the microphone from her.

This is my story.

My heroism.

"Let me tell it."

21

Skyscraper

Skyscraper.

He felt the shaking in his fingers, forced them into balls at his sides. Clenching his eyes tightly, he held back the flow of invading memories. The tremors cut to his heart.

I have to.

Wind shot past him as he rocketed into the air, racing towards the collapse. Shaking tears shook his body as he buried his emotions, pushed through it.

Remember last time.

There were people dying.

Now was not the time.

As his muscles strained to hold together the building, he couldn't muster the strength to fight off the memories any more. Trauma surged, reminding him of the last skyscraper, the one that had collapsed with him inside, given him his powers even as he watched his loved ones die under the rubble in slowed time.

He didn't know how to use them then. He did now. It would be better.

He was their hero this time. And that meant he couldn't bow

to fear.

And then it crumbled.

22

Heroes 2.0

"Rise, we need you."

I nodded silently, watching the faces of the team in front of me. My voice hoarse, I asked, "It's back, isn't it?"

Grim nods answered me.

So I nodded too, grabbed my scythes, and said, "Let's go."

Two weeks later, the dragon began testing us. Fire would rain down from the sky, just high enough to scorch the roofs of skyscrapers. Choking smoke would fill the city. Statues began to crack down the middle, symbols of our legacies being stolen.

"We're fighting for that," Ghostcaller told me once, standing around an oval table with the team. "We're fighting for legacies. For memories. We're finishing what they started."

I met her eyes, a deep defiance lighting in me as I said, "We're not ending it the same way they did."

She knew what I meant. She'd lived with the same pain I had. Her father, torn from her when she was just a kid. My age.

I thought she would understand.

Mara, our water-powered friend, leaned on the table. Rain-drops circled her hands and her body, forming a constantly moving outline of water.

"We're going to do it right this time," she told us, brushing a hair out of her face. "We can strategize. We can beat this."

I nodded in agreement. This would be the last fight. I wouldn't make another team face this. Not again.

"Raven," I called, watching the boy standing against the far wall alone. "Any news?"

He nodded slowly, still swiping on his phone. "The satellites are detecting the dragon. Half a day out."

I paused, then looked back at Ghostcaller. "Are you ready, Suze?" I asked her quietly. I knew better than anyone the pain it caused her to use her powers, the lines she'd drawn. I respected it. I respected her for it.

She swallowed, then met my eyes. "More than ready."

And then I watched them fall. All of us.

That first fight with the dragon was one of epic loss. My blades sang through the air as I channeled more finesse and power into each hit than ever before. The dragon smacked me away easily. Ghostcaller pulled in the power of a long-dead villain, attempted to freeze the breath in the dragon's mouth, but then it inhaled, sensing the power, and absorbed it. The claws on its feet became knives of ice, sharper than steel. Its breath was a storm realized, a blend of ice and fire.

Raven raced into the fight, blazing through the skies, and *punched* that dragon in the jaw. It stumbled. But it didn't fall.

It wouldn't ever fall.

As I dug my way out of the rubble, a woman stood beside me—one I hadn't met before. She offered me a hand. Then she whispered, "Whoa," met my eyes with a scared expression, then quickly glanced away. For a moment I was concerned, then she hummed a quick note, and my spirits lightened. *Maybe we could do this.*

I jerked back, ripping my hand away. "The Songhero," I whispered, almost in awe. Awe is what I'd had before she'd let my brother die. Before her influence had convinced him it was okay to fight that battle. Before she'd been wounded and they hadn't even begun Soar's final fight.

Before she left him.

I shook my head. Grabbed my scythes. "I'm fighting." It was as much an invitation as it was a buried accusation. *I don't leave even when things get hard.* Blood marred my suit. Cuts burned on my cheek. And yet I was still here, still fighting. I gave everything to ensure I was there for my team. She didn't.

We charged towards that beast together, each carrying the weight of grief in our attacks. I carried the burden of legacy, the silence of remembrance. She struggled under the weight of responsibility, the choice of life and death. Failure.

Our blades met across the dragon's head. It went silent. For a moment, I thought we'd won.

"Ghost!" I screamed as the breath began to quicken, as I felt its pulse in my blade. "Do something!"

Then the blast rocketed us backwards.

Dust buried me like a dead man as rocks tumbled in. The building was demolished.

We'd never expected the dragon to get this close. Not today.

"Mara!" I shouted into the radio. We were saving her. A last resort.

But we were all about to die.

She was already on her way, riding the downpour that opened up from above as the pipes burst below us. Water ripped into the street with brutal efficiency. Shook off the rocks lying around me. Tore into the dragon's scales like a high-speed torture device.

With a wave of her hand, a slice of water cut into the dragon. It shook it off, then went to smash her down. She crashed into the street, then everything went silent. The waters were quieted.

She rose into the air, glowing blue, fists clenched with a deeply human rage. The downpour turned to a hurricane, winds ripping into buildings, shoving everything around. She hovered in the midst of it all, unmasked, perfectly still. One silver hair, once blond, rested in front of her eyes.

No.

I knew what she was doing.

I wrapped my blades around the streetlight, took a running start, swung myself in a circle, and raced through the air. Winds pushed and shoved, forcing me to redirect. I shot through the air like an arrow, fighting to get there before.

But even then, I watched her body surge forward as she let go, channeled all of the water into a spike, and, with a roar, left all of her power in a glowing blue burst that rocked the city. Water flooded the streets. The dragon roared painfully as it was shoved onto its hind legs, struggling to stand. It ripped through scales like paper, leaving bare patches of stone and legend behind. The dragon wailed.

And I fell.

I dove with her, caught her body, then swung to the ground. Silent sobs racked my body.

Mara. She couldn't be dead. We didn't have enough time.

Why'd she sacrifice? Why would everyone sacrifice and leave?

The dragon was roaring again. Scales reformed over wounded bones. It was healing. And we were hurting.

Ghostcaller landed beside me silently. Her eyes met Mara's cold, silent gaze, and I watched something in her snap.

"Look away," Suze whispered. My closest friend. The Ghost-caller. "Please, James."

I nodded silently. I couldn't bear to watch any longer anyways.

Even as I gazed towards the distance, I heard a quiet, harsh command in an inhuman tongue, then watched a purple form rise out of Mara. I'd watched this before. But not her. Please. Not her.

"Suze." My eyes met hers. "Please. Not now."

She shook her head slightly. "I'm going to end this." Silently, the two heroes reached out towards each other, until as the Ghostcaller's hand met the spectral figure, their screams split the night. She was reliving Mara's most painful moment.

After a moment of silence, the Ghostcaller shook her head, opening her eyes, looking forty years older. She raised her hand, and the water answered. It rose into the sky, forming a wall of water that could take down anything.

And then, just to make sure, a purple spirit walked out in front of it. Mara.

I watched Suze shut her eyes tightly. Barely felt her hand reach out and grip my wrist tightly. I swallowed, lifted a silent prayer.

I watched as she rose an army of the dead, each one a shade of purple, following Mara's ghost.

And I shut my eyes as they fought.

It was long, I was told. Not bloody, because they'd been given the gift of not bleeding again.

And they hadn't even won.

The dragon had left, leaving city blocks in its wake. Destruction stretched for miles. The ghosts dissipated, off with the mists. And I tried to forget.

After that, our team grew. Mara was replaced like she'd never existed by a 40-year-old accountant who'd fallen victim to faulty tech during a bank robbery. His hands were strengthened by energy, like a lightning bolt channeled into a person. Each step was two, blinking him in and out of space unconsciously. He could teleport at will.

But he wasn't Mara, and I couldn't forget that.

Raven scoffed when we met a college student, mid-20s, who went by the name of the Pigeon and wore a bird mask along with a feathered suit. We all stifled laughs until he whistled and a flock of birds the size of a small car high-tailed it into the building, bursting through our window.

The next arrival was quiet. Reserved. Her name was whispered only in rumors and references to old legends. The Nighthawk. Queen of Kills. Queen of Silence. They said her throne was built on those who had challenged her. Said she slaughtered anyone in her way with a cold detachment. Said she killed without a trace.

Her short, recently-dyed white hair was her way of trying to turn a new leaf. But it couldn't hide the lines etched in her face, the exhaustion, the pain. Couldn't erase who she was.

One day, while the others were arguing around the table, I launched myself out of the window just like I'd seen Soar do a thousand times. The wind blazed through my hair, leaving it standing as I arced through the skies. My brother's cloak, now resting on my shoulders, missing its hood, followed me. I'd left it for a while. But I needed something to remind myself of heroism.

Be the hero, it whispered.

But sometimes I felt the cloak asked for things I refused to give. Sacrifices I wouldn't make. I wasn't Soar.

The cloak was burnt, scorched at the ends. He went out in a blaze.

Controlling my descent with a well-aimed blade, I landed gracefully beside the Songhero. Alone on a cloudy day, sitting on an apartment building. Alone.

"Hey." Her voice was quiet, broken. "I'm sorry." Tears hovered at the edge of each word.

I didn't comfort her. Didn't put my arm around her. Didn't tell her it would be okay.

At this rate, it wouldn't be.

But I stayed with her. And I listened.

"They died," she whispered finally. "My team. We were so powerful. Before Soar came along even. We held the city together. And everyone knew it.

"I was spared. I don't understand it. It was my job to keep them alive, to keep them strong. I stood in their circle, guarded their closest secrets, whispered encouragement in their weakest moments. And they fell around me, one after the other. Not all at once. But I watched each one die."

We were silent for a while after that. Then, she added, "I don't think that's an apology. It wasn't fair for me to leave. I wasn't injured enough to justify it. But I couldn't *bear* to watch more heroes die. Couldn't bear the burden of not saving them. Couldn't bear the reminder that they wouldn't be here if I'd kept my friends alive." She shook her head. "I couldn't."

"I get it."

I didn't smile. Just stared up at the skies. Fighting memories no one would ever see. Wrestling invisible beasts. Grieving my brother when it felt like I was the only one who remembered who he really was.

It was quiet.

Maybe too quiet.

Not a breeze, a car horn, or a bird call.

"This feels wrong," the Songhero whispered, eyes gone soft and light, hands lifted towards the sky. "There's a different chord. An unfamiliar melody."

"No," I whispered, already knowing what was coming.

And then the world split again.

The dragon raced down from the heavens, tearing a rip in reality. Words of legend and stones of statues spiraled around it as it dove. Pages of history books melded together formed its wings. It fed on legacies. And it was here for ours.

"Go!" I shouted, acting on instinct as I shoved the Songhero out of the way. Seconds before the gaping mouth and shiny teeth crashed into the roof, I snagged my chain blade on a crooked fang and yanked myself above its head.

The earth felt slow as I raced back down, headed towards the beast's back.

I angled myself, bulleting past the beast and swinging back up with my scythes, arcing over the monster's head. Audio crackled to live in my ears—the Ghostcaller's terrified voice. "James, where are you?"

"Right here." The words came out breathlessly as I danced through the air, blades spinning and cutting, trying to hold the beast still. My brother's cloak billowed behind me, catching the wind with burnt edges, accomplishing nothing but remembrance. A familiar silhouette. But he'd lost. And I couldn't win this. I had no powers. But I could try.

I heard a soft voice singing melodies, felt my hits grow stronger. The Songhero was working.

"Suze!" I shouted, calling to the Ghostcaller. "Please." The dragon's tail smacked me down into the building again. I felt it shake below me as a curved claw, sharper than a sword, pressed into my chest. The dragon growled.

And then the world broke. Again.

In a roaring crash, the building collapsed under me. Dust flew up in all directions as I fell, the one thing I promised I'd never do, set to meet a fate I swore I never would. Death. I watched the Songhero fling herself off the collapsing apartment building, heard her voice grow louder and her song wrap around me. Every scrape from rubble healed instantly. My last moments would be painless, at least. Strong. But I couldn't do anything.

Then a flock of pigeons swept through the rubble, expertly dodging like trained pilots, and saved my life.

We landed on the next building over, next to the Songhero and Suze. The Ghostcaller's eyes were filled with purple and the rock at her feet was cracking and shifting in a small circle.

"You're not allowed to die yet, silly!" she laughed, her voice echoing like she wasn't really here.

The screams still filled the air. People lived in those buildings.

Before I even registered it, I'd shoved Ghostcaller, broken her connection. I punched her in the face, knowing she deserved a lot more, then dove off again off the side.

My blades danced through the rubble. I snagged a little boy, probably five, who was sobbing as he clung to the side of a collapsing level. Then a teen girl, resting at the bottom, covered in dust and scrapes, with another stone a foot above her face. I delivered them, then dove back in.

This was heroism.

Even as the dragon terrorized above, I ignored it. I had to focus, or none of us would make it out alive. The building was still shaky, still liable to cause more damage at any moment. I'd pulled another twenty-two people from the rubble, working quickly as my hands shook.

She wouldn't have done this.

The last one was unsavable. A quiet heartbeat that stopped in my arms. A little boy's golden hair that would never be combed again. My cloak settled around him, just like it did to Soar when he fell. I tried. I really did. But he was dead.

And I couldn't reverse death.

I wasn't sure if I was hurt, angry, or what when I pulled myself back up to the ledge where my friends stood. The Ghostcaller's eyes were purple again, and her hands puppeted a giant blade made out of the rubble. Dust followed her every move as she sliced in the air, mirroring the sword that swung towards the dragon.

"How many died?" Her voice was quiet. Haunted.

"Seven." I shook my head. "Should've been none."

"We would've lost more without you," she whispered, eyes still locked. Quickly she twisted her wrist, reshaping the sword into a reflection of the dragon. A clone that roared with purple eyes and a slowed movement.

The dragon ran.

I would've too.

"I wasn't worth that." That was the first thing I said when we sat in the meeting room again. The team was silent. Songhero—I learned her name was Alex—hummed slightly, wrapping lyrics around my wounds. "They shouldn't have died," I continued.

"She made the right call." It was the Nighthawk. She brushed her hair out of her face, now covered in dust. I hadn't recognized the silence. But she was in that rubble with me.

Slowly, the others began to nod. Pigeon added, "Rise, do you know how many would've died if you did?"

I traced the lines of broken trust from face to face, my unbelief growing. "You can't be serious."

The grave expressions on each of their faces told me otherwise.

78

Finally, the Ghostcaller spoke up. Not the apology I expected. Not even an excuse.

"The last heroes died trying to save everyone. If we want to win this, we have to be brutally efficient." She caught each one of our eyes. "A life for a life is meaningless when you have the potential to save a thousand more. We only sacrifice when it's worth it."

Silence. Heavy silence.

I didn't disagree. But she wasn't right.

No matter how much I hated his sacrifice, Soar's hadn't been in vain. But it wasn't worth it. No life was worth trading. Ever.

And no hero should ever end an innocent person's life.

Every strategy meeting after that felt detached. We shared the same beliefs. But the differences felt so vast.

"We'll call on their villains," the Ghostcaller explained after another attack, after the casualties of another ten people. The dragon was gone. For now. "Those spirits can strengthen me and they can tell us how to beat the dragon. The heroes didn't win. But the villains would've given anything to win."

Quiet murmurs of agreement echoed around the room. Villains. It could work.

I shook my head. I knew where this was going.

And yet we stood in a cemetery, watching Ghostcaller kneel before the graves of the wicked. Long-buried bones that should've been left alone. And yet she called forward their spirits, eyes glowing purple as her skin glowed with an unearthly hue. This wasn't just drawing on their powers. This was them.

"Heroes." The word came out like a curse. A whispered accusation from a voice that should not have been this clear.

Darkwing. They called him an angel of death. Working in the shadows. Bringing only pain. Phantom wings spread from his back, and his fingers were sharpened into blades.

"How do we defeat this beast?" Ghostcaller asked, a faintly proud smile growing on her face as the purple spirit flowed from her palms.

Darkwing gave a quiet chuckle. "How do you think the rest of us escaped? Die."

Ghostcaller's face turned in a moment, her smile vanishing and her expression souring.

Watching her, Darkwing added, "If death couldn't kill it, what makes you think you could?"

With a flick of her wrist, the spirit dissipated like mist, and she moved on.

Villain after villain. None of them had an answer. She connected with each of them, absorbing their abilities. Her eyes took longer to return to their normal brown each time. Her screams of pain grew quieter, but more broken. And every time she returned from a memory, fingers crackling with some new ability, all I could see was her spirit breaking, one piece at a time. The pain she was going through was destroying her.

Next came the heroes. The old ones, but they never were as famous as this generation. Then the Songhero's team. I watched Alex flinch away, her hand shaking as she held it to her face, unable to look. Next was the Ghostcaller's dad. He'd fallen with Soar in the final fight, racing around the battlefield like a bullet. The pain of his death had brought the Ghostcaller her abilities. I couldn't see why she'd summon him now.

After his spirit faded and he had nothing to say, she turned to me, voice soft. "Don't stop this."

My breath caught. "You promised." Instinctually my hands drifted towards my blades, but I resisted. This was someone I'd called a friend.

A sad smile. Then, "We need him."

"He didn't even have powers!" My voice was louder than it needed to be, echoing through the graveyard, splitting the night's silence.

"He was a leader." She was quiet. Resolute. "I need that."

I shook my head. "I know how your powers work. And his pain isn't yours." She would see his most painful moment. The instance that had wounded him the deepest. And I didn't want to know what it was.

I couldn't know. Because I knew it would break me.

"Susan, don't." My voice was layered with a violence I never thought I'd hold for her. A quiet threat that I was sure she caught.

She shook her head sadly. "I'm sorry."

And then Paul's spirit began to rise from the next grave.

At first, he looked just like himself, only this time formed of purple smoke. It was the same easy grin he'd worn in life, the same outfit he'd donned for every fight, the same blue blades by his side. His cloak floated behind him, carried by an ethereal wind, now complete and unmarred.

And then he saw me.

The smoke rippled as he turned, locking eyes with me. "James."

My breath seemed to stop. Tears pricked my eyes. It was *him*. My brother. Back for a moment.

"James, it's back." His voice held a fear I'd never heard in life. His eyes revealed a terror that shook me to my core. "Run."

I stood, frozen.

I watched her.

She reached out, hand trembling, towards Soar, towards my brother, towards his most painful memory.

And before I'd even recognized it, I tackled her. An inch away from her ruining my life. We crashed to the dirt as I landed blow after blow on her, tears racing down my face, sobs threatening to choke me, thoughtless fists hailing down. "You promised," I gasped in between sobs. "You wouldn't." My voice turned harder. "It wasn't yours to take."

The world shook. A deafening blast shook us, but I kept fighting, tears streaming down my face. I felt a flame on my back, a heat that I couldn't contain. So I kept punching.

When they pulled me off of her, she was bloodied and bruised. I was exhausted, everything in me gone from that moment of passion. I collapsed onto the ground, chest shaking. Knowing that I'd stop her again in a heartbeat.

And in that moment, our friendship died.

Kneeling in the dirt, I was numb. The world seemed silent. Or maybe I'd given up listening.

My brother's cloak rested in my hands. Just a few scraps left, still burning away with a purple flame. It licked my fingertips, burning slightly, but I didn't move. Just sat there, silently, watching his legacy burn away.

It was all I had left. Everything I had.

And now it was gone, just like him.

Hands shaking, I reached into the dirt as the last of the cloak burnt. The ash lay in an outline on the ground—a cloak, the silhouette of a fallen hero. I nearly cut myself as I took my scythe to my shirt, cutting off a sleeve with jagged edges, then folding it together.

The Ghostcaller knelt beside me. Didn't say a word. Just took the strip of clothing for me, folded it neatly. Then she pulled out a soft, purple twine, grabbed my scythe, *Soar's scythe*, and threaded it together. A pouch.

Tears streamed down my face like a forgotten waterfall as I

gathered the ashes, formed a pile, scooped them up, and gently carried them to the pouch. I would remember this. I couldn't forget.

Once they all were gathered, I wiped my face, grabbed the pouch, and forced myself to my feet with a strength I didn't know I had. *Don't fall.* I nodded slightly towards the ground, uncertain if it was a message to my brother, his legacy, or myself. Or to a world that had scarred us both.

I refused to fall.

The next battle was quiet. But everything seemed dull when compared against the overwhelming, blinding loss that I was experiencing again. A loss of memory, a twisting of heroism. A betrayal.

We drew the dragon to an empty forest. Trees burned, fell, shook the earth as their roots failed them. Every hit I made felt echoing, each attack less precise. Each fall felt brutal without the soft presence of my brother's cloak. His final memory, shredded.

When the dragon smashed me into the earth, I barely felt it.

Broken. That was how I felt. Not the same. Not even right. Not normal. Messed up.

I knew exactly why. And I knew I could never forgive her.

Each attack, from pigeon armies and silence that collapsed spirits and ghosts that should never have been awakened, from songs that raced across battlefields and scythes that sliced deep, from the final-sounding echo of Raven's punches—each attack was worthless against the beast. We were losing. And we would die as losers.

"What did they do last time?" Pigeon asked at our regrouping behind a rock formation. My fingers lingered by my side, brushing against the pouch that held my final memory.

I wouldn't die like him. That was all I knew.

"They died." My voice broke halfway, revealing a human weakness that I wished I could escape.

"We have to." The Ghostcaller's voice was steady, sure. She didn't sound like she was deciding our team's fate. Didn't sound like she was sentencing us to death.

"Blazing final stands." Raven forced a smile, but I could tell the idea hurt him. "Not a bad way to go out."

The rest of the team slowly nodded in agreement. I locked eyes with Alex, the Songhero. It seemed almost like I could hear her thoughts. *I won't let them die without me*, she swore internally, so I knew, even though it pained her, she'd agree.

And then the world lit ablaze.

We heard the dragon's roar, too close for comfort, a second before a light like the sun blinded us. When I could see again with shielded eyes, I watched a flaming figure race through the skies, going toe-to-toe with the dragon that ate legacies.

I could hear Alex's smile in her voice. "The Burned One. They can't take his soul if there's nothing left."

He'd given it all away before. And somehow, without emotion, he'd still known we heroes needed a hero.

I felt the rippling heat even from here, and it only seemed to grow hotter. We launched ourselves into battle next to him, determined to take this beast down together. My scythes wrapped around the dragon's exposed fang as it roared, and I swung with the chain, opening my wings to glide onto its back.

This would be it. I could feel it.

The Burned One—Sam, my brother had called him, one of his closest friends—fought in an eerie, soulless way. He didn't flinch at incoming danger, just calmly moved at the last second. His motions were calculated, precise. His attacks were strategic, aimed at the beast's eyes, then its mouth as it roared.

He didn't die. And that's why they won.

And then he died.

I watched Raven get too close, one of his punches landing on the dragon's jaw. The beast stumbled, then snapped its teeth— but the Burned One was already there. He held the dragon's mouth open as his flames grew only hotter. I stood on the ground for a moment, unsure of what to do, watching the black scorch marks spread across the dragon's maw. I could see the fear in its eyes.

And then it bit, and the Burned One exploded. It knocked everyone back, sent a wave of heat that scorched every plant in a thousand yards.

We hit the dirt and burnt grass, digging shallow graves into the soil from our impact. Graves like he would never get. Graves like Soar never got.

I caught Raven's eye, placed my hand on his shoulder, and I could feel him tremble. I could see the horror in his eyes. He'd just killed a legend.

We were dangerously close to the edge of a cliff. I'd nearly fallen, only saved by my blades. The chasm stretched below us, threatening to claim our souls..

"It's time." The Ghostcaller looked as if she'd seen a ghost. But she was more resolute than I'd ever seen her.

I shook my head violently, hand clenching around my scythe's comfortable grip. A memorial of sorts. A weapon I'd made my own. A legacy retold. I fingered the pouch on my left side, feeling the weight of memory inside.

They were only memories because he had left me. Soar had fallen.

And that's when I swore I would rise.

One by one, the team stepped forwards. I watched as they

drew on power beyond comprehension. Raven's eyes darkened, his hair turned to feathers, and time seemed to slow around his movements, almost like he was out of sync. His hands rippled, shaking reality around them.

The Ghostcaller had an echo around her, her purple spirit, larger than she was. Smoke surrounded her, the spirits of countless others at her beck and call.

The Pigeon's eyes were full of remorse as he let out a low whistle and the birds within a thousand miles responded, flocking in by the hundreds, then the thousands. An army prepared to die.

The Nighthawk did nothing different. They already called her a goddess. But it felt like she slowed down, just slightly. Like she was out of sync with the world. And she looked happier because of it.

The Songhero whispered a note that split reality, that echoed with a chorus invisible to the eye. Her soft words rippled with power, like they could command the nature of a person, not just heal them. A soft smile grew across her face. She knew this would be her end, but I think she accepted that.

I stood still. The last human.

"James." The Ghostcaller took a careful step towards me. The dirt sifted under her feet, leaving footprints in her wake. Purple smoke rippled into the air towards me.

"I don't have powers," I answered simply to her unasked question. "I can't do that."

She nodded, slowly. "But you'll sacrifice, right? Just like your brother."

Be the hero.

In that moment, my fists clenched, and I knew that Soar was wrong. It wasn't heroic to die. I'd thought that before, but now it was an unshakable truth, now that I faced the fight myself. It wasn't an impossible trade. And I knew I was making the right choice.

Just like your brother. I met her eyes with cold defiance. Hatred that she dared to use him to convince me. Hatred that she broke me.

"No."

The word seemed to have power that I didn't. Everyone froze.

The Ghostcaller blinked, once. A tear slowly rolled down her cheek.

"Then I'll have to sacrifice you."

Before I could react, before I could draw the blades at my sides, my hands snapped to my chest. A purple echo of me rose, and it felt like death. I could feel the pulling, like I was being split apart. I could feel the forgetting, as I lost who I was, as I lost who my brother was.

When they die, without me, who will fight?

But I didn't have a choice. A silent scream ripped from my lips as smoke surrounded me, obscured my vision. A cold palm pressed against my collarbone. My friend. Once.

I was falling. I couldn't rise.

I was dying.

Then a beautiful scream saved me. It rippled with a thousand voices, with the power of an army. The Songhero's melody, woven from her own soul, carrying the healing power that she'd used so many times before, but this time having unlocked a darker, deeper side. A hurting power, because sometimes hurt was required for healing.

The blast shot us back as the air reacted to the Songhero's broken call. Her melody commanded nature itself with a will so powerful that the wind cracked in a rush to obey. The cracking sound echoed throughout the silence before the blast sent me flying through the air, sent the Ghostcaller flying towards our team.

Falling.

The wind wrapped around me, whispering notes that I could feel within myself. The pouch ripped open, and I felt a tear race down my cheek, knowing my final moments would be spent in the loss of my brother's final memory.

And then the ashes began to move.

The Songhero's voice only grew louder, more powerful, as she changed notes, added defiance and power into her words. In an act I knew I could never understand, the ashes wrapped around me. They formed the delicate cloak I remembered, but this one was different.

It was mine.

Feathers formed of legacy and ash shot down each side, divided by a cut in the middle. When they caught the air, they solidified, lifting me up. Helping me rise.

I hovered before my teammates. Caught the Songhero's eye.

She was too far gone to turn back now.

As I realized they were walking to their deaths for a fight they wouldn't win, I finally had the courage to step away. "You're already dead," were my final words, words that carried an accusation. They weren't the heroes they should've been.

They would fall.

But I would rise.

23

Fate

They fell.

I watched the screen, just like thousands of others, as the news helicopters recorded live the fall of the second heroes. Heroes 2.0, the city had called them. The new generation. Our saviors. The dragon fed on legacies. On memories so strong they screamed for attention. For heroes so pure that they became something... else. On what heroes crafted every day, in every choice. It fed on legacies.

The first generation had been pure. Protectors. The Vanguards, they called themselves. Heroes of insane power and quiet dedication. And yet they fell. But they banished the beast. Made it flee. It was gone for a while.

When it came back, it met a different breed of savior. The city christened them Heroes 2.0, but they didn't have a name. Just broken promises and spirits. The new generation was efficient. Brutal. They sacrificed when needed. Did what they had to do. The beast was gone now. But so were they. And I knew the beast would return. But they wouldn't.

When I told my mom my plan, her eyes went wide with

fear. Her hands started shaking—that familiar tremor she'd developed after the building collapse, one I thought was long gone. "No." Her words shook with a broken authority. One that refused to let someone else die.

Not after Alec died.

But that was why I had to do this. Without a hero, I would be dead too.

But without a hero, I wouldn't have watched my little brother die in someone's arms.

I had to be my own hero.

"You're a child!" she exclaimed finally as her shaking slowed. "I won't let you. You're too young. This isn't for you." Her eyes lit with a defiance that stopped grown men in their tracks. When my mom wanted something, not many things could stand in her way.

Luckily, that was genetic. I felt my fists clench, my brow furrow, the grief flooding through me again—but this time, it was accompanied by purpose. "I'm eighteen." It came out as more of a snarl than a correction. "I'm in charge of my life. You don't get to stop me anymore."

"I get to stop you when you're making a stupid decision!" Her eyes flashed. "This is going to get you killed."

I nodded slowly, voice quiet. "It might. I know."

But I couldn't handle life without action. Fate had relegated me to an observer, a civilian to be protected. It was time to choose my own fate.

Sometimes when I lay in bed at night, staring up at the ceiling, that memory replayed in my brain. The floor shaking a half-second before the cracks started. Then in the blink of an eye, it crumbled, and I started falling. My heart would pound in my chest as my fingers reflexively echoed the movements, reaching for rocks that would cut me, walls that were already breaking, something to hold myself to.

And then finally my hand closed around Rise's. His arm wrapped around me, and his blade snagged the side of a wall. Powerfully he yanked, pulling us out of the collapsing building. Leaving me on the ground, he smiled faintly, then launched himself back into the mess.

There were twenty-two of us alive. My mom. My dad. Me. Our neighbors.

Seven were dead.

Including Alec.

I'd watched Rise hit the ground beside me, my little brother clutched in his arms. His golden hair was a mess, going every direction. We were going to get a haircut that afternoon. He wore a blue button-up shirt, having just come home from church. That wasn't what we buried him in.

Tears were streaming down Rise's face—not one, not two, but a waterfall of grief. I knew it broke him.

And then I watched him hand the body to my mom, his hands shaking, and then return to the fight.

In that moment, I knew I wanted to be a hero. No matter what life was in store for me, I knew I didn't want it anymore.

And as I lay there remembering, I knew I had one thing to do.

Find Rise.

My uncle looked at me with haunted, sad eyes when I asked him. "I've watched too many heroes die, Peter," he told me quietly. "I know what you want to do. And you're too young to do it."

"I'm not," I shot back stubbornly. A fire was growing in my chest—a blaze of repeated words. *Too young.* "It's my life. I'm just taking control of it."

He shook his head sadly. "Then I'm not helping you."

When I asked his coworkers at the news station, they told me the same thing with quiet words and painful, memory-filled expressions.

"Besides," one added, "no one knows how to contact Rise. He just appears when we need him."

None of them understood. I didn't want powers. I wanted a choice. I wanted to step in instead of watching. To fight instead of being fought for.

So I kept looking. I showed up at their old headquarters day after day, waiting for the last surviving team member to return. Nothing. I started showing up at crime scenes—little things, like house burglaries. I'd watch from a distance as Rise stepped in, but I was never fast enough to catch him after.

Until the day I cornered him in the alley.

Rise stepped out of the shadows. His cloak was lined with scarlet feathers. His cheek was marred by a white scar. He looked broken, haunted. But I knew he was still fighting.

He gripped the scythe's handle tightly as he closed his eyes and told me his story. The story of his brother, Soar, falling to the dragon. The story of this new team, of their moral collapse, of how he'd tried to fight anyways. The story of how he stepped away. The story of the choice he made to keep fighting for good. I listened to it with an awe and respect. He didn't choose heroism, no; not in the traditional sense. He was encouraged towards it. But if he hadn't had the character he did, the strength he did, he wouldn't have stepped forward. A lesser man would've let someone else take Soar's place. Rise couldn't imagine that. It was his burden to bear. And then he chose to keep fighting.

And I respected that.

"Was there anything left of their legacies?" My voice was

steady, quiet. The notebook rested against my side, forgotten. The bricks of the alleyway against my back cast a shadow over us, hiding us.

Rise sighed. It sounded broken, like a soul snapped, or a chord with a missing note. "The dragon absorbs legacy," he told me, echoing what the stories said. "It comes for the strongest. For the heroes." He shook his head. "There's nothing left from them."

"From the dragon, maybe?"

Rise met my eyes. Paused, like he was about to speak. And then he saw the resolve, and he nodded slightly. "One thing. We left it there. It's buried under the Pit. Didn't want to touch it."

"Thank you." A smile found its way to my face, lighting up my eyes. Finally, someone understood this drive. Someone helped me decide my own fate.

"I'm sorry." Rise's words were soft, like he didn't know why he said them. He tightened his grip on a scythe at his side.

"Thank you," I repeated. "You saved me once from the building. And you just saved me again."

Because that day, something shifted. The defiance wasn't aimless. I could change my fate. I could fight the future promised to me. I could be a hero, not a bystander.

I turned to walk out of the alley, then jumped as I felt Rise's hand on my shoulder. I didn't even know he'd moved.

"I'll come with you," he told me quietly.

When I walked beside Rise, I watched the people's reactions. Citizens would step out of his way, giving slight bows of respect. Speech would go silent, replaced by hushed whispers. He commanded a presence. He strode through crowds, nodding at people, smiling.

They respected him. Because of his choices.

That was true power.

When we made it to the Pit, where Heroes 2.0 fell, where they tried to sacrifice Rise, I watched his facade collapse. His hand trembled by his blade. One hand was wrapped in the cloak on his back. Quietly he hummed a quiet song, the notes floating through the air.

"This is where we fell."

I found it interesting that he included himself in that. We stood beside a cliff, marked with lines across stone. A blast circle, ten feet wide.

It was where they tried to sacrifice Rise. Where he'd had to leave them.

"Down there." I followed Rise's finger down the edge of the cliff, towards the forest below. This place had been destroyed. Fires scorched the trees. Fallen logs covered the ground.

In the middle of it all was an empty pit, hollowed out by sheer power.

That was where they died.

We slid down a slope to the side, and he led me to the Pit.

"This is where they gave themselves up. Sacrificed." His voice was harsher now. "I told them not to."

I nodded slowly. I'd seen the footage. The entire city had.

"I've only been here once," he continued. "The day after. I had to see if there was anything left. Had to-" He stopped, turned away, and wiped his tears. "There wasn't."

His knee hit the ground, and he carefully began scooping dirt out of the way with his blades. A small flower was thrown to the side. Beneath it was a single stone, rounded perfectly. It glowed faintly blue, and it was covered by lines of handwritten text.

"This was what the dragon left behind. A single stone of swallowed legacy." He set his blades beside him in the dirt.

94

"I wouldn't touch it."

It wasn't an insult this time. Just a warning. Not a command.

"But we all make our own choices," Rise finished. "So here's yours." He met my eyes. "My life is hard, Peter. But it's worth it."

I nodded. My hands shook. *Why were they shaking?*

I could die here. I knew it before. But it seemed different now. A wave of realization. Fear gripped my heart. I could hear my blood pumping.

And then, a chorus of voices.

"Too young. Too dangerous. It's not for you."

So I reached out. Hands trembling. Heart racing. Sweat rolled down my brow as I reached out *and touched it.*

I controlled my fate. Not the other way around.

And I was done with giving up control.

The world went blue.

It stank of pain as I watched humanity's lifespan race by faster than I could blink. I watched blasts of otherworldly power replaced by dead silence, watched heroes fall and be replaced by villains.

My skin.

It *tore* at me, *ripped* outwards, not my skin, no, not me, the blue did. Draconic power, legacy embodied, the pain of a thousand memories. They shoved outwards, splitting me apart.

My eyes went wide as I let out a blood-curdling scream of pain. I felt my knees hit the ground, felt myself collapse, felt my head hit the dirt, felt my body shake.

I felt pain.

My eyes flashed with images. A haunting silhouette. A dragon, built of *stone* and *legacy* and *memory.* I heard the cries of those who went to fight it. Felt the same power in it, the same pain, that existed now in me.

Except I chose this. And I chose to fight for good.

Even as it destroyed me.

The power danced under my skin, begging for release, pushing against the fabric of my being. It was too much to contain in myself. Too many stories ended, untold, or forgotten. Too many legacies to count. Too many stories contained only in tears and whispers.

I'd never felt more alive.

When my vision cleared—not back to normal, no; it seemed everything was still tinted blue ever so slightly—Rise stood over me, watching. His face was soft. His mask was off.

"You're okay," he whispered, kneeling down beside me.

My body shook with pain, with power I couldn't hold.

If it hurts, it worked.

It worked.

I was different.

No longer just human.

Not superhuman. Something different. Something *more*.

I was a hero. A being defined by choice.

And that meant I didn't bow to anything.

Because I controlled my own fate.

24

Architect

"Archie." My voice trembled, broke, *shattered*. I was watching my own best friend, my brother without blood, die before my eyes.

And he just wanted to sacrifice more.

Rise couldn't help here. So I took off the mask, became James again. This was my friend. Not my teammate.

"Archie, you can't," I repeated, watching his screens. We'd had this discussion before. Too many times.

The monitors were alight with cameras from triangular drones, hunting through the city or battling criminals. Each wave—there was five—was being controlled by a thirteen year old boy, sitting in his office desk with a VR headset. Sweat rolled down his brow as his hand shook slightly—a tremor. That hadn't been there last time. Coffee cups and energy drinks were all around, filling his trashcan and crowding his workspace. One hand danced with a pencil and a paper, sketching out the design for a large, human-shaped exoskeleton.

"I have to," was his simple response.

"You're thirteen." Every word felt like I was losing him

already. I closed my eyes, clenched my fists, and I was back, pretending to not hear Paul's quiet, shaking sobs, pretending not to watch the exhaustion he carried every day, the silent knowledge that it was all going to end. Before he sacrificed.

No. This would be different. I wasn't thirteen anymore. I had a say.

Archie spun in his chair, now facing me, but still fighting another battle I couldn't see. His hand tapped anxiously at the air, and he whispered, "Exactly." Then, louder, "I'm thirteen. If I can help now? That's extraordinary. That's necessary."

"You haven't even been a kid!" I argued, knowing it wouldn't work. He didn't care about anything other than the people.

"James." Archie's voice got quiet, serious. "Without me, the city would be destroyed. If I stepped down, everything would shatter. People would die. *You* would die."

"You don't deserve this."

"If anything, this is the best option for me." I could hear the smile on his face without having to look. "James, I'm incredible! Every thought I make saves lives. Every decision I weigh rescues a broken person. I'm a hero. I'm the Architect. I'm designed to keep building." Archie sighed, set down the headset. "When I didn't? People died."

I sighed, slamming my hand on the desk beside him, perhaps a bit harder than I meant. But the idea of losing him? That *shattered* me. How was I supposed to survive in a world where I'd let this kid die?

If he fell, it was on me.

"You don't have to sacrifice," I told him, voice more confident now. "This fight isn't yours. It's mine. This is my legacy. Not yours."

He paused for a second, and I was sure he was meeting my

eyes. "This is my city," he told me quietly. "And that means I fight til my final breath."

I shook my head. "No. I won't let you," I swore. To myself. To him.

"You don't get to make that choice." His voice carried the calm, calculated tone of an orderly mind, but behind it, I heard a trembling kid, voice shaking from fear, exhaustion.

One of the screens went black, and I watched him flinch, watched the reaction on his face of intense pain, watched how his fists clenched and his knuckles flushed white.

It was destroying him.

"I'm okay," Archie finally mumbled. "I've gotten stronger. I added a chip to help me offload the crime-hunting. I just handle the battles now."

A second later, a flash of white filled the screen, and I heard the whirring of drones as another ten took off down the streets of the city. Off to save lives, hold buildings, and issue warnings. Off to be heroes.

"The dragon is coming," Archie whispered quietly. We both knew it. It had come before. We had lost before. "That's why you're here, isn't it?" he asked.

I nodded slowly.

"You stopped me last time." A hint of malice lined his voice like a blade. "And they all died. I'm not letting that happen."

"You can't die." I wasn't sure if it was a plea, a bargain, an order. But I needed him to agree. Desperately. I needed this boy to agree to live, because I didn't know if I could survive another loss. "Please." A shattered voice, filling the room like a flood. One word that broke us both.

"I might." The thirteen year old's voice was still. He seemed at peace. It made no sense.

We sat there in silence. I didn't know how to try to understand his philosophy. Sacrifice like that? That was stupid. It wasn't on either of us that they died. But he didn't see that.

A quiet pause filled the room as he continued to battle.

"Archie." My voice carried a new confidence. I knew the root of his problem. "You love people too much."

He scoffed, then swiped in the air, switching one of the screens to a new fleet of drones. Waiting on me to elaborate.

"You forgot how to love yourself," I continued, growing more brave. "You love with every inch of you. But if you keep going like this? You're falling apart. You need to care for yourself. You love them too much."

"Yeah, maybe," he admitted. "But without an Architect, who's going to fix things?"

I shook my head. "Sacrifice isn't the way. You're leaving a void that you're forcing someone else to fill." *Maybe* that *will get to him*, I thought. If not himself, then remembering his people, those people he fought for. Realizing that just like Soar, he would find someone else to take the fall, to be the hero. It had happened to me. I didn't want that for anyone else.

A little half-smile. The same one I remembered seeing when we'd met when he was twelve, when he'd started all of this. "James, sacrifice is noble. Sometimes destruction is needed for redesigning."

25

Ashes

Heroes 3.0

* * *

"You'll all die." I met each of my teammates eyes, ensuring they would understand. Them. Not me.

Each of them knew my stance on sacrifice. That wouldn't be changing.

"Then we'll die together," Peter decided.

"That's stupid." I couldn't keep the scorn out of my own voice. "Sacrifice means you'll leave the city without its heroes. I'm not enough to stop everything. You can't leave me." My voice cracked slightly, betraying my emotions.

Not them too.

Please, God. Don't let them die.

Artemis sighed, and the trees breathed with her. "If we must, then we will. Without us, there will be civilian casualties. Do you really want that, Rise?"

I shook my head slowly. "Of course not. You know that. But-" Flashes of my brother's face filled my mind. That horrible moment when Soar had fallen. The moments of horrible silence that had filled the *after*. The worst time of my life.

And then the attacks that started.

I'd had to take up the mantle. Alone. Powerless. Because everyone else died.

And civilians died because of that, too. I could barely stop a mugging, or a kidnapping. What use was I when an alien army stormed the city?

Each of us had risen to fill that void. But I didn't want to force a new generation to take on my curse.

So I would survive. I would keep fighting.

"We'll need new suits!" Archie shouted excitedly, drawing me out of my thoughts. The young boy already had a notepad out, with a dozen drones surrounding him, each offering different art materials. The Architect, they called him. Another of us who'd had to step up when everyone else was dead. His robots were remarkable and his talent was unmistakable. But he shouldn't have had to suffer for everyone else.

I would fight with them. But I would keep fighting.

When Archie brought me the suit, I met his eyes for perhaps a moment too long. Tears filled my vision as I pictured him falling, pictured the 'heroic' sacrifice they'd all tried to sell me on. Pictured it taking this boy's life.

Nanotech suits. Impressive, but it wouldn't stop their deaths.

The suit activated itself, standing up in front of me as an empty shell. I breathed deeply, then stepped in. It wrapped around me. The suit bore my insignia, an eagle of red with blue-tipped wings, emblazoned in metal. Magnets allowed me to snap my scythes to my sides, readying them for a moment's notice. My cape, formed of violently red feathers, split down the middle, clung to my back. A reminder of what I'd lived.

Rise. My promise to myself. I would never fall. Never sacrifice my life, like my brother did. Because I'd seen firsthand just how much pain that brought.

It wasn't heroic. It was selfish escape from a world where you had failed.

Perhaps their abilities blinded them, made them idealists. I was the most human of the group. I still walked amongst the people we saved, still felt their struggles and weaknesses. I was still one of them.

Even Archie was becoming one with the machines; the chip he'd implanted in his neck was connected to his bots, controlling them with a thought. But sometimes, I feared, their logical directives would win out over his emotions.

I fought to remain human. And I fought for humans.

When we stood on that street, the sun at the perfect angle to cast deep shadows behind us, I felt alone. I was with a team of heroes. My team. And yet I knew I would be the only one to survive.

And it would be so much harder after.

My cloak rested against my back. A reminder of everything I'd lost. The team that had died without me. The team that had tried to kill me. My brother that abandoned me to saving the city.

The wind lifted the back of my cloak, and it solidified, becoming wings that stretched out behind me. Like an eagle. Because I rose.

As the golden triangle opened in front of us, as the otherworldly beast floated through, I glanced at my teammates, telling them one final goodbye. "I love you guys."

And then the fight began.

The beast was like a dragon, slithering like a serpent, but made of twisted metals, cracked stone. Fallen memories. A purple fire lit it from inside.

It was forged from its victims.

It fed on legacies.

It had killed my brother. Destroyed his team. The first Vanguards fell. Will, the man of flame, sacrificed everything in order to lock it away, to destroy it, or so we thought.

It killed my friends. I didn't know if it did, or they did. But they were never the same after it arrived. And they died like that.

I didn't think it could be killed.

The legends said it followed power. Arrived when heroes reached godhood. When they grew too powerful, too adored.

The power of superhumans that had transcended humanity met the scales of a beast that was forged of an inhuman hatred. Trees snapped, withered in an instant. Massive ghostly blue chains wrapped around its limbs, only to snap in a silent echo. An army of a thousand bots dove at it, only to be eaten in an instant.

But they kept going. More bots swarmed out of the streets, replacing Archie's lost followers. I bit my lip, watching as Archie activated his own suit, leaving the ground beside me to rocket up next to his creations. Artemis hissed in fury, then clenched her fists, forming her own monster out of rock and dirt. A humanoid creature, towering twenty feet tall. A dwarf against this monster.

Peter's eyes narrowed. This was why he fought; I knew that. And he looked ready when he raced into the air, armor crackling with blue energy, curved blades forming in each hand. His energy raced along the ground below him, slamming into the beast, crafting another set of chains to tie it down. Peter slammed into the dragon with his blades, sliding down its side. The beast roared, swiping paws through the air. It couldn't hit Peter.

But it could hit someone else.

"Archie!" My blades danced like second nature. I hooked onto a drone, then another, then the edge of a scale, pulling myself up towards the boy in a desperate attempt to save him. I shut my eyes, not daring to watch the dragon's claw racing down anymore, trusting instinct to kick in. The wind raced past me, slamming into my wings, giving me the boost I needed as I shot out my arm, wrapping the blade around Archie, and fell to the ground.

I breathed out slowly as I anchored myself to a nearby building, slowing our fall to a casual swing. *He was safe.*

For now.

To beat this monster meant giving yourself away.

My plan would have meant more casualties, likely. Would've meant more deaths. But it would have saved a thousand more in the years to follow. Years where heroes remained to fight for the people.

We could've chained the beast, held him down for another ten years, then repeated. But that wasn't enough. They told me it would break the chains eventually. People would die. Best for it to be them.

It wasn't the best.

Gritting my teeth, I promised myself that I would fight until I had to back off. I would try and see their plan through. Some unheard of way to kill it could exist. We would try everything. So I wrapped my blade around a building corner, launched myself into the sky, and dove down towards the dragon. With spinning scythes, I cut deep into its face, slicing down as I slid.

Swinging on the chain, I left the blade embedded so that I could land a devastating kick to the beast's neck. It stumbled, which unhooked my blade and sent me falling gracefully back towards land. My cape caught the wind, the synthetic wings helping me soar, just like my brother, but just like me. They folded back together, going limp without wind, as I landed gracefully beside my team.

I glanced at them. "Let's go."

Peter nodded, lowering his helmet, and then forged a blue spear and screamed a war cry. As he leapt through the air, I watched his figure grow ten times, an avatar of blue energy that echoed his every move. The ghostly spear drove down into the dragon, which lurched, then coughed painfully.

A glimmer of hope. *Could we win this?*

"No," I heard Archie whisper in horror as the cuts on the dragon's face reversed. The monster rose to his feet, every blow we'd managed seemingly undone.

"Plan B," Peter shouted as he crashed into the pavement next to us. A thin layer of blue smoked around his armor, marked with the distinct claws from this dragon-like monster.

"No," I whispered, echoing Archie from before.

Plan B was the sacrifice.

As my team rose into the air, each of them crackling with otherworldly power, I let up a quiet prayer that God would somehow reveal a different way.

Archie let the energy take over, surrounded by a giant mech that snapped into place around him. With a robotic arm, he pointed forward, and ten thousand robots swarmed around him. He shot into the sky, blocking the sun for a moment, and raced towards the dragon.

Peter's eyes were full of unleashed chaos, as his entire body spasmed, as blue energy crackled over his skin. His weapon changed every second. The avatar he formed wasn't him, this time; no, it was the beast itself. A smaller version. His version.

Artemis rose a few feet into the air, levitating as the trees and the earth bent to her call. Rocks floated around her, forming a massive sword. Grass grew at an insane rate, wrapping around the dragon a hundred yards away, tying it to the ground. Her skin slowly covered over with bark, and she stiffened, freezing into her final position.

Each of them let out a war cry simultaneously, like creepy echoes from sources I didn't recognize. None of them sounded real; each was a cheap imitation of the real person, a rocky scream, an echoing yell, a robotic cry.

Then they charged.

I launched into the air after them, spinning between Archie's bots and the blasts of fire the dragon-like being launched. Purple fire. Almost the hottest.

Peter's weapon, now an axe, embedded itself in the dragon's side. A blue explosion rippled out, sending me off course and slamming into a wall. The other champions were unaffected.

But Peter was nowhere to be seen.

Desperate, I threw myself through the air, spiraling past my other teammates to the spot where Peter had fallen. My heart stopped, and I felt like a giant palm stopped my progress midair. It felt like I was falling, but I wasn't sure if I was.

I'd known he would die, but to see our leader's body on the pavement felt so *wrong*.

In that instant, Archie and Artemis landed their final blows. The blast rocketed me into the side of a building, which collapsed under the impact, burying me inside.

"No." Tears streamed down my face, but I didn't have time,

not now, so I kept pushing at the rocks until I found a path out. I pulled myself out, bruised and battered, with the scythes my brother had given me. The scythes that were now worn and bloodied. The scythes that had gone through war.

The dragon looked wounded. Its once terrifying stare now showed genuine fear as it breathed in deeply, like it was trying not to collapse. Each of the wounds still glowed with other-worldly power.

They'd given themselves up to their powers.

"No," I decided as I watched the dragon turn, breathing flames on a crowd of civilians. Even if they didn't listen to me, even if they betrayed me in death, I wouldn't let their sacrifice be for nothing.

I landed between the beast and the crowd. Biting my lip, wiping away a tear, I launched myself at the beast, blades sharp and spinning. I cut into its flank, then yanked myself over its back, slicing into its stomach, then pulled myself around to slice at the mouth. Around and around I went, dealing relentless damage, watching black blood pour out, until finally, the beast collapsed.

Maybe it would've collapsed anyways.

I stood in the horrible silence again, breathing heavily.

The dragon made one final roar, raised its head to lock eyes with me, and I caught a glimpse of raw power still hidden within those eyes.

And then I felt it.

The next roar was like a wave, like a force, a law of nature. Everything went white, like a blizzard. I could feel the power unravelling me from the inside out, erasing my identity. Trying to erase my heroism.

Good luck, buddy. It's all I am.

Fight me.

Blindly, I lashed out with my blades, feeling them embed in the dragon's head. I shut my eyes tightly, blocking out the horrible light, resisting that horrible feeling that I could feel in my gut. Like a rollercoaster. Like a nightmare. My wings shot out, reacting without wind for the first time, wrapping around me like a protective shield. A legacy. A promise. *I won't fall.*

For Soar. Paul's face filled my mind. His never ending smile. *Be the hero.*

For the team. Archie. Peter. Artemis.

For the people. Everyone I'd ever connected with.

In the end, I think those connections saved me. They anchored me to my humanity. The human hero.

If my humanity couldn't be taken, then they'd never take my heroism.

"I won't die." The words were ripped from me brutally. A declaration, an attack on the dragon, a refusal. Sacrifice was stupid. And it wasn't how this would end.

When the blast was gone, the dragon was dead.

And no one remembered.

It was just gone. The street was still scorched, the building still destroyed, but the people walked around like it was an ordinary day.

And every day that passed, the evidence of the event faded more and more. The building was rebuilt. The street was repaved.

But they didn't remember us.

They didn't know what a hero was.

I was still a hero. I'd survived. Some would say I lost. But I survived to fight another day.

They'd forgotten.

But I remembered.

Forgotten. Maybe it was mercy; blessed to never watch another team rise and fall to this beast. Maybe it was curse; left to be the one who remembered, suffering because I survived.

Whatever it was, it meant this was it. I was the final hero. And I hadn't fallen.

The Hideout

The Hideout.
It's the beginning of something new. A place for normaheroes to gather, talk, and share their own stories. A place for

discussions, fan theories, and community.
It goes beyond this book. It's a mission. It's a story just beginning.
Normalheroes is my origin story. If you want to be there for what's next,
you'll want to scan that code and join now.